Music in Bali

Music in Bali

EXPERIENCING MUSIC, EXPRESSING CULTURE

LISA GOLD

New York Oxford
Oxford University Press
2005

Oxford University Press

Oxford New York
Auckland Bangkok Buenos Aires Cape Town Chennai
Dar es Salaam Delhi Hong Kong Istanbul Karachi Kolkata
Kuala Lumpur Madrid Melbourne Mexico City Mumbai
Nairobi São Paulo Shanghai Taipei Tokyo Toronto

Published by Oxford University Press, Inc.
198 Madison Avenue, New York, New York, 10016
www.oup-usa.org

Oxford is a registered trademark of Oxford University Press

Library of Congress Cataloging-in-Publication Data
Gold, Lisa (Lisa Rachel)
Music in Bali: experiencing music, expressing culture / Lisa Gold.
p. cm.—(Global music series)
Includes bibliographical references and index.
ISBN 0-19-514150-4—ISBN 0-19-514149-0 (pbk.)
1. Music—Indonesia—Bali Island—History and criticism. 2. Balinese (Indonesian people)—Social life and customs. I. Title. II. Series.

ML345.I5G65 2004
780'.9598'6–dc22

2004041563

Frontispiece: Gong with ornately carved stand showing Bhoma, demon protector.

Printing number: 9 8 7 6 5 4 3 2 1

Printed in the United States of America
on acid-free paper

GLOBAL MUSIC SERIES

General Editors: Bonnie C. Wade and Patricia Shehan Campbell

Music in East Africa, Gregory Barz
Music in Central Java, Benjamin Brinner
Teaching Music Globally, Patricia Shehan Campbell
Carnival Music in Trinidad, Shannon Dudley
Music in Bali, Lisa Gold
Music in Ireland, Dorothea E. Hast and Stanley Scott
Music in the Middle East, Scott Marcus
Music in Brazil, John Patrick Murphy
Music in America, Adelaida Reyes
Music in Bulgaria, Timothy Rice
Music in North India, George E. Ruckert
Mariachi Music in America, Daniel Sheehy
Music in West Africa, Ruth M. Stone
Music in South India, T. Viswanathan and Matthew Harp Allen
Music in Japan, Bonnie C. Wade
Thinking Musically, Bonnie C. Wade
Music in China, J. Lawrence Witzleben

Contents

Foreword

In the past three decades interest in music around the world has surged, as evidenced in the proliferation of courses at the college level, the burgeoning "world music" market in the recording business, and the extent to which musical performance is evoked as a lure in the international tourist industry. This heightened interest has encouraged an explosion in ethnomusicological research and publication, including the production of reference works and textbooks. The original model for the "world music" course—if this is Tuesday, this must be Japan—has grown old, as has the format of textbooks for it, either a series of articles in single multiauthored volumes that subscribe to the idea of "a survey" and have created a canon of cultures for study, or single-authored studies purporting to cover world musics or ethnomusicology. The time has come for a change.

This Global Music Series offers a new paradigm. Teachers can now design their own courses; choosing from a set of case study volumes, they can decide which and how many musics they will cover. The series also does something else; rather than uniformly taking a large region and giving superficial examples from several different countries within it, in some case studies authors have focused on a specific culture or a few countries within a larger region. Its length and approach permits each volume greater depth than the usual survey. Themes significant in each volume guide the choice of music that is discussed. The contemporary musical situation is the point of departure in all the volumes, with historical information and traditions covered as they elucidate the present. In addition, a set of unifying topics such as gender, globalization, and authenticity occur throughout the series. These are addressed in the framing volume, *Thinking Musically,* which sets the stage for the case studies by introducing ways to think about how people make music meaningful and useful in their lives and presenting basic musical concepts as they are practiced in musical systems around the world. A second framing volume, *Teaching Music Globally*, guides teachers in the use of *Thinking Musically* and the case studies.

The series subtitle, "Experiencing Music, Expressing Culture," also puts in the forefront the people who make music or in some other way experience it and also through it express shared culture. This resonance with global history studies, with their focus on processes and themes that permit cross-study, occasions the title of this Global Music Series.

Bonnie C. Wade
Patricia Shehan Campbell
General Editors

Preface

I took the preface photograph of this book at a *mecaru* (exorcistic purification) ceremony in Sukawati village in 1992. You can see in the foreground a daytime ceremonial shadow puppet performance in progress, surrounded by people praying and watching. A shadow master manipulates the tree of life, a rawhide puppet that embodies the spirit of this ancient storytelling genre and forms a link between him and the world of the stories, accompanied by musicians seated at instruments behind him. Also shown are gongs from another music ensemble played, often simultaneously, to summon, entertain, and ward off evil ground spirits, the main purpose of this villagewide ritual. As in many Balinese ceremonies, this one is not devoid of onlooking tourists.

The most striking thing to me about this ceremony, aside from the colliding simultaneous sound worlds and noisy, crowded atmosphere, was that it took place in the major intersection of an extremely congested north-south route, requiring people to redirect traffic, halting the ongoing pace of daily life in a visceral way. In this annual ceremony the entire village participates in a multistaged ritual to cleanse the village, ending with a villagewide procession to the sea, thus enabling village life to continue undisturbed. People have had to adapt this ancient ceremony to the modern world, surrounded by exhaust fumes and tourists, but it is no less powerful in its intent and function. This book introduces you to some of these juxtapositions, beginning with my first impressions.

> *Bali was not what I had expected. Upon landing at Denpasar International Airport in 1981 I was whisked away in what felt like a high-speed chase up winding roads to the village of Peliatan, my home for the next year. As I stared out the back of the* bemo, *an open truck with benches that was*

Wayang lemah (daytime ceremonial shadow puppet play) from a mecaru (purification) ceremony in Sukawati, Gianyar.

the major form of transportation then, a blur of sights, sounds and smells enveloped me through the exhaust fumes. People seemed to be moving both incredibly quickly and slowly. Mainly, I was amazed at the sheer numbers of people everywhere. Motorbikes and other vehicles passed us, sometimes while oncoming vehicles were doing the same, my driver narrowly avoiding collision numerous times. Once we left the city we passed through villages that seemed to be lined up along the main road so that the traffic path whirled through, disrupting a much slower flow of people in their daily activities. We passed open food stalls with people seated on benches, people doing laundry in the irrigation ditch that ran alongside the road, others washing chickens or bathing in the same ditch. As we passed through the village of Mas, known for its mask carvers, signs in front of many houses marked wood-carving galleries, painters, textile sellers, and antique dealers. These signs in English, clearly aimed at the tourist market, masked whatever else lay behind them.

Where was the Bali that I had been dreaming of for so many years as a gamelan student in the United States? The Bali of anthropologists and music researchers from the 1930s, in whose writing I was steeped, was portrayed as a tranquil paradise, a kind of communal utopia. This image was immediately dispelled upon encountering the linearity of the road cutting through traditional life as I had imagined it. But I was not easily disillusioned and was prepared to seek out the "real Bali."

The next day I was taken to a village of I Nyoman Wenten, one of my music teachers with whom I had studied in California, and found what I was looking for. In celebration of the inauguration of a new gamelan musicians and dancers were invited, many of whom I had had the honor to study with in the United States. Dozens of people crowded into courtyards of the small family compound to eat while dancers adorned themselves for the performance. Seated on woven mats on the ground, they helped each other dress and put on makeup and gold flowers in their hair, from small children to older adults. Once the performance began in the village com-

munity center structure, it struck me that gamelan *was just a tiny fragment of the cultural mosaic, as my focus flitted from one image and sound and smell to the next, feeling a wonderful sense of confusion at being surrounded by the unknown. Over the course of the year, as I became immersed deeper and deeper into this world, closely living and working with performers, Bali became less "exotic" while every ceremony seemed richer in heartfelt beauty than the last. At the same time, the more I learned, the more I realized how little I understood. Admitting this is the first step toward allowing a place to be real.*

In this volume you will learn that there is no single "real Bali," but that there are many ways of perceiving life in Bali. You will need to be aware of this society's centuries of feudalism resulting in a hierarchical society layered onto its collective one, of the impact of Dutch colonial rule, the national Indonesian government's influence, and the onslaught of tourism and pollution. But I want you also to experience another aspect of modern Bali, showing links to a pan-Southeast Asian cooperatively based lifestyle and worldview whose religion honors its natural surroundings, its rice cultivation, and group musical practices, in addition to its own syncretic practices.

My Balinese music and shadow puppetry teachers, with whom I have studied for over twenty-five years in the United States and in Bali, have shared with me their most generous, patient, and energetic spirit, as well as their incredible expertise in a highly developed, complex musical art. For them, giving to others, whether through teaching, passing on knowledge, or performing for family and community, is the highest valued form of fulfillment. Naturally there is danger in seeming too simplistic when I say that I found this spirit to be present throughout Bali, and that Bali indeed *is* magical in many ways. I ask that you try to see Bali's multifaceted, far from utopian reality, but not be afraid to allow yourself to succumb to its wonders.

A NOTE ON SPELLING AND PRONUNCIATION

There is variation in spelling in Bali (just as there is in musical practice). I have chosen to adopt the *pa, ma,* or *ba* spelling of prefixes (otherwise seen as *pe, me,* or *be*) because this is widely accepted by linguists and Balinese and is closer to the transliteration of the Balinese characters. For instance, I use *balaganjur* rather than *beleganjur*, and *pagulingan* rather than *pegulingan*. In pronunciation the vowel sound is swallowed so it sounds more like a contraction (*b'leganjur* or *p'gulingan*). The letter *C* is pronounced as *ch* unless there is a cedilla under it, in which case it sounds like an *s*, as in *Çudamani*.

Plurals do not have an *s*, so in most cases I have chosen to omit the *s* unless it is unclear to do so, such as in *gangsas,* where I want it to be clear that I am referring to more than one instrument.

ACKNOWLEDGMENTS

I wish to thank deeply all of my Balinese teachers, for whom teaching and learning is cherished. I am indebted to I Dewa Putu Berata, his family, and the members of Sanggar Çudamani, the gamelan group you will hear on most of the examples on this book's CD (see list of performers). Dewa led the gamelan in the recording, advised me in the planning of examples, and made the illustrations for this book. His analytical mind and helpfulness as a teacher, composer, and performer proved invaluable in this project.

In a book with limited scope such as this it is possible to acknowledge only a fraction of my many teachers in the body of the text, so I will try to do so here. Deep thanks go to Wayan Loceng and family, Wayan Rajeg, Nyoman Sumandhi, Komang, Putu Sutiati, Ketut Yasi and the Tunjuk *gender* ensemble, Wayan Konolan, Wayan Suweca, Ketut Suryatini, Wayan Sujana, Nyoman Sudarna, Made Lebah, Niluh Sriyathi, Nyoman Windha, Ni Gusti Warsiki, Ketut Arini, Nyoman Cerita, Ni Dayu Diasthini, Ketut Kodi, Desak Made Suarti, Nyoman Catra, Dr. Wayan Dibia, Made Wirathini, Ketut Gede Asnawa, Wayan Nartha, Made Subandi, Wayan Wija, Andrew Toth, Dr. Wayan Rai and Ibu Sri, Dr. Made Bandem, Wayan Sinti, Ibu Nilawati, STSI, Made Arnawa, Nyoman Sutiari, Made Sija, Made Sidia, Dr. Nyoman Wenten and family, Richard Wallis, Emiko Susilo, Michael Tenzer, David Harnish, my fellow gamelan musician friends, Gamelan Sekar Jaya and its many teachers, and all of my other close friends.

I thank those who gave permission to use recordings (listed in CD Track List), Eliot Bates for mastering the CD, Sheila Huth for assistance in preparing the index, and all of the readers who gave me valuable criticism, including all of my students at Colorado College and UC Berkeley. Special thanks go to Made Lasmawan and his family, Victoria Levine and the Colorado College music department, Pat Campbell, and the editors at Oxford University Press, Jan Beatty, Talia Krohn, and Lisa Grzan.

Deep appreciation goes to Bonnie Wade, coeditor of this series, mentor, and friend, for her insight, support, and careful reading, advice, and patience through the many incarnations of this book.

I thank my parents, siblings, in-laws, and Maya and Omri, who have always encouraged me. I thank Devon, for constantly reminding me of the most important things in life. And finally, to my husband, Ben, for support, encouragement, valuable feedback, recording and other technological help, insights, criticism, patience, and love.

CD Track List

Unless otherwise noted, all recordings are field recordings of the gamelan group Sanggar Çudamani, recorded with permission by Lisa Gold and Ben Brinner. Special thanks to I Dewa Putu Berata and the gamelan group Sanggar Çudamani from Pengosekan Village, Ubud, Gianyar (listed below) and Wayne Vitale for permission to use Vital Records excerpts.

1. Night sounds
2. *Gamelan gong* playing a temple piece with priest's and congregation chanting in distance (field recording from Tatiapi, Gianyar, 1990).
3. *Gamelan gong* playing the *gineman* (introductory section) of the *lalambatan* (slow temple piece) "Jagul" (I Dewa Alit, *trompong*, Sanggar Çudamani).
4. *Gamelan gong* playing the *pangawak* (main body) of the *lalambatan* (temple piece) "Jagul" (I Dewa Alit, *trompong*, Sanggar Çudamani).
5. *Gamelan gender wayang* in *wayang lemah* (daytime ceremonial shadow play) performance during a ceremony (*Gender wayang* performers from Kayu Mas, Badung, Denpasar, include I Wayan Konolan and I Wayan Sujana; *dalang* [shadow master] Ida Bagus Ngurah Buduk).
6. "Topeng Keras" (accompanies a strong *topeng* characer).
7. "Topeng Arsa Wijaya" (accompanies a refined character).
8. *Gamelan gambuh*: *gineman* and dramatic excerpt illustrating stylized speech (Batuan *Gambuh* ensemble, Vital Records 501, track 1, "*Batel*" *selisir* mode, with permission).
9. *Gamelan balaganjur* playing a processional *gilak* piece.
10. *Gamelan balaganjur* playing a *kreasi* (new creation) for procession (Sanggar Çudamani).
11. *Gamelan gong kebyar* "Jaya Semara" complete version (Sanggar Çudamani).
12. *Gamelan jegog* Werdi Sentana, "Jegog. Bamboo Gamelan of Bali" CMPCD 3011, 1991.
13. The "wave" of paired tuning.

14. Three pentatonic scales in the *pelog* tuning system.
15. Listening to the gongs.
16. "Jaya Semara" demonstration, building up layers; structural framework of gongs; low instruments; *ugal; gangsas* and *reyong.*
17. Drums: syllables spoken by I Dewa Putu Berata, then a pattern played on two interlocking drums.
18. *Gangsa kotekan norot* (single-note interlocking).
19. *Gangsa kotekan nyog-cag* (leaping interlocking).
20. *Pangecet* (final) section of the piece "Jaya Semara," alternating between two types of *gangsa* interlocking.
21. *Kotekan telu* from the piece "Jauk Manis."
22. Same *kotekan* as in track 21, played at a faster tempo.
23. Same *kotekan* with full gamelan.
24. Expansion and contraction of a *kotekan empat* (4) pattern, from the piece "Teruna Jaya."
25. *Ocak-ocakan reyong* alone ("Teruna Jaya," Sanggar Çudamani).
26. Same excerpt with full ensemble ("Teruna Jaya," Vital records, 401 with permission).
27. *Reyong* syncopated interlocking patterns from "Topeng Keras."
28. *Reyong norot* interlocking from pangecet "Jaya Semara."
29. *Gineman* and beginning of "Sekar Sungsang," a "sitting piece" named after a kind of flower, played on *gender wayang*. Tunjuk *gender wayang* musicians: I Nyoman Sumandhi, Pak Sukantri, Pak Winatha, and Pak Nengah.
30. *Batel* (a colotomic meter used for action scenes).
31. *Omang Barong* (a colotomic meter used in Barong dance drama).
32. *Bapang* (a colotomic meter).
33. *Gabor Longgor* (a colotomic meter, here used in "Jauk Manis").
34. *Gilak* (a colotomic meter used for processions and "Topeng Keras").
35. "Topeng Keras," layering demostration.
36. *Kecak,* the "Monkey Chant," a sequence of forms and melodies.
37. *Kecak,* a 16-beat melody.
38. "Sinom Ladrang" played by Sanggar Çudamani.
39. "Jagra Parwata" (The Awakening of the Mountain), *Kreasi Baru* for *Gong Kebyar* by I Nyoman Windha (Vital Records 402 [1996], with permission).
40. "Pengastukara" [We Give Blessing], a new composition for *gamelan semarandana,* composed by I Dewa Ketut Alit, performed by Sanggar Çudamani.
41. *Gamelan angklung*: two excerpts of a field recording from a *melaspas* cermeony inaugurating a house temple in Pengosekan, Gianyar; *kidung* chanting is heard in the background.

Musicians in Gamelan Sanggar Çudamani, Pengosekan, Ubud, Gianyar:

Dewa Putu Berata
Dewa Ketut Alit
Dewa Nyoman Sugi
Dewa Putu Rai
Dewa Made Suparta
Dewa Ketut Alit Adnyana
Dewa Putu Sudiantara
Dewa Putu Wardika
Dewa Made Swardika
Ida Bagus Made Widnyana
Ida Bagus Putu Aridana
I Wayan Sudirana
I Made Sukadana
I Kadek Armita
I Koming Wirawan
I Nyoman Sudarma
I Gst Nyoman Darta
I Made Suandiasa
I Ketut Surya Tenaya
I Made Widana
I Made Karmawan
I Made Mahardika
Gst Putu Ratna
I Made Supasta

Sanggar Cudamani Dancers in Legong Photos:

Dewa Ayu Eka Putri

Gusti Ayu Suryani Dewi

Ni Wayan Febri Lestari

CHAPTER 1

The Balinese Ceremonial Soundscape: Simultaneity of Soundings

Imagine yourself sitting outside on a warm Balinese night, breathing in the fragrant air of flowers, incense, and spices. The intense heat of the day is fading away as crickets and frogs loudly make music of interlocking rhythms in the nearby flowing stream. The sounds of a Balinese night are like none other as the coolness awakens all senses with high-pitched energy. Even the insects join in this awakening, their constant buzzing of musical pitches from low to high providing another level of sound to an already complex fabric (CD track 1). Over the glowing water of the nearby rice fields wafts the sound of a distant *gamelan,* a musical ensemble of bronze gongs, metallophones, drums, and flutes, being played at a local temple ceremony. A pair of wooden slit-drums of high and low pitches, hanging from the temple tower, are being struck in Morse code–like patterns, summoning local villagers to come to the temple and give their offerings. Such sounds compose one of Bali's "soundscapes," an entire sound world of which "music" as we know it is only one part.

Gamelan. *The word* gamelan, *borrowed from Java but widely used in Bali, translates as "musical ensemble" but implies certain kinds of indigenous Javanese and Balinese ensembles. The Balinese* gambelan, *from* magamble, *"to strike," denotes the playing technique of many* gamelan *types; however, it has come to include ensembles of instruments with other playing techniques (such as flutes) as well (see chapter 2). The term, depending on how it is used, can*

mean the sets of instruments themselves or a particular group of players. Although it is possible to speak of individual instruments in a gamelan, *it is a collective term used for an entire set of instruments that is made by one* gamelan *maker and tuned together as a set. As sets of instruments, there are some thirty distinct types in Bali. It is difficult to count the exact number of varieties because new ensembles are constantly created and older, nearly extinct ensembles are revived. The number of musicians in a* gamelan *can range from as few as two to as many as sixty musicians. Notice the different timbres from one gamelan to another on this book's CD. Each gamelan has its own unique timbre and feeling, even among ensembles of the same type.*

Each type of gamelan *has a name denoting the instrumentation and repertoire (*gamelan gong kebyar *or* gamelan gender wayang, *for instance). Additionally, a group of players may take on its own name, thus reinforcing group identity, and often using imagery from nature, such as flowers, in combination with vibrant modifiers. Some examples are* Gamelan Tirtha Sari *(pure, essence of holy water),* Gamelan Gunung Sari *(pure sacred mountain), or* Gamelan Semara Ratih *(the names of the male and female love deities).*

Gamelan *are most frequently made of bronze, bamboo, or both, and less frequently of iron. The most ubiquitous* gamelan *is often referred to as* gamelan gong, *or abbreviated simply to* gong, *indicating the great importance of the gong in most ensembles. It is the gongs that link Bali's* gamelan *to Southeast Asia's widespread ancient tradition of gong forging and its association with spiritual power and community.*

In Bali, as in many places, the concept of "music" is context-specific. Rather than a single category called "music," or "song," numerous types of *gamelan,* repertoires (groups of pieces that are linked in some way), and vocal practices are named and associated with the specific functions that they fulfill. For instance, one form of vocal chant is sung by a shadow puppet master when he brings a character to life, while others are used for narration, dialogue, or to express moods. A congregation of worshipers bonds as a community and with the spirit world by singing a different form of chant. Another form of chant is sung in reading clubs by specialists who interpret esoteric texts by first singing the poems in their archaic language, then improvising solos that paraphrase them in the local Balinese language, thereby bringing the ancient texts up to date. No single term encompasses all of these vocal activities. Likewise, instrumental music stands in a distinct category from vocal music. Borrowed from Java, the term *karawitan* (meaning "in the state of refinement") is the adopted umbrella term for playing *gamelan*. Each musical ensemble, form, technique, and vocal genre carries with it intrinsic ideas about context, mood, and meaning and is usually linked to dance and theater forms. I will use the term "music" to include indigenous *gamelan* and vocal performance. Please note that while Western imports and influences such as jazz and popular music exist in Bali (the term *musik*, borrowed and adapted from English, denotes these), I will not be including these in my discussion.

In this volume I take you to a number of performance contexts in which you may encounter music as it is heard in its soundscapes and glimpse the associations that music conveys. Listening to each CD example when it appears in the text will help you begin to experience Bali, at least from a distance. This chapter introduces you to the main themes of the book while providing contextual and historical perspectives on Balinese worldview. A visit to a Balinese temple ceremony permits a brief look into Bali's present and past through the living arts of performance. Chapters 2 and 3 delve into the inner workings shared by many forms of Balinese music. Chapters 4 and 5 take you to the heart of Balinese performing arts through dance and theater, and the final chapters explore musical form, preservation, and change. You will see that contemporary Balinese performance, when viewed in light of its cultural and historical context, provides a window into Bali's variegated and rich past as well as its participation in a modern, globalized society.

Three themes recur and intersect throughout this study to guide you and remind you of the ideals and values most cherished by Balinese practitioners. I say "ideals" because sometimes there is a discrepancy between theory and practice. In a place such as Bali, where the temptation of visitors is to romanticize, it is important to view these ideals in light of a larger organic whole. The themes presented here, therefore, provide guidelines to be evaluated and questioned throughout the book.

Theme 1. Balinese music is primarily an ensemble tradition, reflecting the value placed on group identity over individual expression and also reflecting, to a certain extent, the cooperative nature of Balinese social organization.

Theme 2. Music, dance, theater, and ritual are completely integrated. Poetry is sung and stories are told through music and dance. Ensembles are linked to dance forms and to enacted narratives. Music itself is inherently theatrical, with the ability to move a community and shape a ritual event.

Theme 3. Contemporary performing arts are intrinsically linked to Balinese identity and sense of history. Through performance, the past is played in the present.

To give you a sense of why these themes are important, I take you on a visit to a temple ceremony (an *odalan)* in Sukawati Village in 1981, my first year of study and life in Bali. My teacher, Pak Loceng, would play in a shadow puppet performance to be held at the temple later that night. Pak is short for Bapak, meaning father, also a respectful address for a male. People have many names that indicate their title, caste, and birth order, thus placing them in relation to the status of others. Of the birth order names for the commoner majority caste, Wayan, Madé, Nyoman, and Ketut indicate first, second, third and fourth born, respectively. Pak calls me 'Dé, short for Madé, as I am a second born, and prefers that I call him Pak, indicating the familial relationship he extends to me as his student.

> *I sit on my music teacher's verandah while he and his family prepare to go to the temple for the annual* odalan, *a "temple anniversary" celebrated every 210 days, the length of a Balinese year). First he and his family will bring their offerings to the temple and pray with the rest of the community. The entire family is dressed in ceremonial clothing reserved for such occasions. His daughter helps me finish dressing by wrapping a temple scarf around my waist, a symbol of purity that enables people to enter the consecrated grounds of a temple. The women of the family have been preparing offerings for days by making rice into colorful cakes that they have dried in the sun and then layered with fruit in an elaborate display several feet high. When all is ready they place the offerings carefully on their heads and walk with a graceful, smooth gait toward the temple. The full moon is reflected on the shiny palm leaves along either side of the dirt road as we*

join the rest of the people from the village on their way to the temple. The headlight from an occasional motorbike or truckload of people going to the temple temporarily silhouettes my companions.

As we approach the temple, the sounds become louder and more complex. A jumble of tunings, timbres, registers, and rhythms resound in a blend that sounds confusing to me. Vendors hawk their wares, some with distorted megaphones advertising cure-all medicines, balloon sellers squawk their balloons to attract the children, cassette vendors play Indonesian pop music loudly over speakers, and throngs of people gather around and move in patterns toward and away from the temple entrance.

Steam rises up from the food stalls, where people sit eating and drinking. Kerosene lanterns dimly illuminate little tables with piles of peanuts and corn for sale. Modern life blends strikingly with something ancient and powerful. From inside the temple walls many sounds emanate through the open sky: a Brahmana priest (of the highest priestly Hindu caste) intones ancient Sanskrit chant while ringing a bell, a practice that formerly was just between him and the gods but now is disseminated to the masses through a distorted P.A. system. Even though the congregation does not understand Sanskrit, they now have come to expect that otherworldly sonority blending with the others because of the changes that modern life has brought about, in this case by using a microphone for something once private. This fades into the distance as we approach a gamelan playing a temple piece (CD track 2).

Crowds of women carrying colorful offerings similar to those of my teacher's family, balanced gracefully on their heads, process into the temple along with men and children also on their way to pray and pay respect to the visiting gods. I follow as my teacher's family joins them. The feeling of community is intense. Even the sounds of the musical ensembles express the spirit of group cohesion. Several different gamelan *ensembles can be heard at once, even though they are separate performances. But nothing in Bali exists in isolation. I notice that there are many focal points for performance within this temple festival, and later I learn that this is because the various performances are for different audiences. They range from the personal, private communion of the Brahmana priest with gods, to group performances done for gods, to performances for gods and humans, and finally, the closest thing to "secular" performance in Bali, performances for humans.*

The coordination of these performances seems loose and arbitrary, yet they all relate to the activities of the priests and congregants in some way that everyone seems to understand implicitly. How do Balinese make sense of all of this? Why is one performance appropriate for gods and another for secular entertainment? What criteria determine the sense of appropriateness?

PLACE, TIME, AND CIRCUMSTANCE

One aspect of life that helps maintain Balinese cultural identity is encapsulated in the Balinese concept *desa, kala, patra.* This expression (roughly "appropriate place, time, circumstance") means that for every activity there is a proper time and place. Place has to do with the natural surroundings and meanings ascribed to spatial orientation. Time is reckoned according to ten overlapping calendars, to which is added the time of day. Circumstance is the particular situation and actions of the individual, family, or community. To know yourself in Bali is to know where you stand in relation to place, time, circumstance, and the rest of the community. This knowledge seems inherent, yet it is acquired by living it. This sense of appropriateness is explored in the next sections.

THE ACT OF OFFERING

The name Bali means "offering," aptly expressing a major component of Balinese life: making, giving, and performing offerings to the gods. These offerings include flowers, incense, rice, fruit, and animal sacrifices, as well as music, dance, and theater. Ceremonies occur daily, in and outside of temples, along the roads stopping busy traffic, by the ocean, and in home compounds. Most religious practices require music of some kind, and it can be heard from great distances. Over centuries these religious practices have undergone changes, absorbing elements from outside cultural influences. Today's *Agama Hindu Bali* (Balinese Hindu religion) or *Agama Tirtha* (holy water religion) is a synthesis of pre-Hindu beliefs and practices with elements of Indian Hinduism and Buddhism, which reached Bali via the neighboring island of Java. Ancestor worship, animism, and the honoring of spirits and deities associated with cycles of nature, such as rice cultivation, link Bali to other indigenous cultures of Southeast Asia.

Religious ceremonies are organized into five categories known as the *Pancayadnya* (from the Sanskrit *panca,* meaning "five" and *yadnya,* meaning "ceremony" or "sacrifice"). They honor the living (rites of passage such as weddings, births, and tooth filings), the dead (such as cremations), sages, demons (such as exorcism), and gods (such as temple ceremonies).

***Odalan* (Temple Ceremonies) *and Ramé* (Full, Boisterous, Active).** Each village or town contains at least three temples: a village temple, a temple of origins, and a death temple. Many others exist, such as a temple for high-caste members of society. Each is devoted to a specific purpose. A temple's *odalan,* celebrated every 210 days (one Balinese year in the Hindu-Bali cycle), marks the anniversary of the day it was first inaugurated. This often coincides with the full moon, but because each temple has its own anniversary, the ceremonies are scattered throughout the year.

Other than during the period of the *odalan,* temples are just empty structures consisting of several adjoining, walled courtyards open to the sky within which are roofed ceremonial pavilions and shrines. During the *odalan* the temple is transformed into a colorful feast for the senses (figure 1.1). Shrines, statues, and pavilions are wrapped in hand-painted gold-leafed cloth. Incense smoke wafts throughout the colorfully dressed crowd and music fills the air. The boisterous, full atmosphere, known as *ramé,* is essential to a successful ceremony and requires the active participation of the entire community. Its opposite, *kosong* (emptiness) or *sepi* (aloneness) is reserved for *nyepi,* one day of the year when no fires are lit and no music is played. It is considered potentially dangerous because demonic forces are drawn to emptiness. People prefer the safety of *ramé.*

The order of events in the *odalan* generally follows this larger structure: a ritual purification and exorcism during which demons are invited to enter the temple and then are escorted out, an invitation to the gods and deified ancestors, an entertainment period of several days, and a sendoff of the gods. Many stages include ritual processions with

FIGURE 1.1 *Temple decorated during an* odalan. *(Photo by Lisa Gold.)*

music delineating spiritually pure and less pure space and time. The congregation, led by priests, presents offerings of food, incense, prayer, and entertainment. In ceremonies occurring within a house a similar sequence is followed on a smaller scale.

Music plays a powerful role of accompanying the ceremony and affecting its dynamic shaping. The word *ngiring* describes music's function as "guiding along" and "accompanying" ceremonial and theatrical performance, illustrating a link in function and association. Music can summon, entertain, or escort out gods and evil spirits as well as accompany humans in various activities, from inspiring processions to inducing trance states or bringing dance and drama to life. Music has the ability to move people as a community and to act as catalyst during important points of ritual change. Obviously, this is not unique to Bali (see activity 1.3 at the end of this chapter).

Spatial Orientation. The Balinese worldview is directly connected to the natural environment of the island. Spatial orientation is of utmost importance and always relative to the volcanoes Gunung Agung and Batukau (figure 1.2). Of Bali's four large volcanoes, the tallest, Gunung Agung ("Great Mountain") is considered by the Balinese the Indian seat of the gods, Mahameru, transported to Bali. Every temple in Bali has a representative shrine at the "Mother Temple," Besakih, located on the side of Gunung Agung (figures 1.2 and 1.4). The cardinal directions are oriented toward and away from the spiritually powerful mountain, determining the placement of things, including music, dance, and ritual activities. Toward the mountain, or "inward," is *kaja,* also the term for cardinal north, and toward the sea is *kelod,* also the term for cardinal south. The closer one is to *kaja,* the closer one is to the gods and spiritual purity. Toward the sea are demonic forces. The east-west axis that follows the path of the sun also has significance. A person feels more at ease sleeping if the bed is arranged with the head closer to the east or north, for instance.

Balinese identity exists on multiple levels, from a national identity as Indonesian citizens to increasingly localized identities as Balinese, town or village members, and as *banjar* (local community organization or hamlet) members. Bali is a province of the Republic of Indonesia, whose motto is "Unity in Diversity." The Indonesian archipelago (figure 1.3), consists of some thirteen thousand to fifteen thousand volcanic islands; the exact number changes depending on the tides. Over half are inhabited by hundreds of diverse cultures and linguistic groups. These disparate cultural groups were unified in 1945, when Indonesia became a nation. Indonesia is now 90 percent Muslim and culturally diverse. Bali remains one of the few Hindu cultures of Indonesia, although that religion was once widespread throughout Southeast Asia. Although small (5,620 square km, population around 3 million), and close to the much larger and more densely populated island of Java (a thirty-minute ferry ride at its closest point), Bali maintains a strong cultural identity and a rich and diverse musical life.

Within Bali, nine distinct regions, roughly based on former kingdoms, have fostered the development of many distinct musical traditions and cultural practices. Before the twentieth century roads were poor, and many communities lived in isolation because of insur-

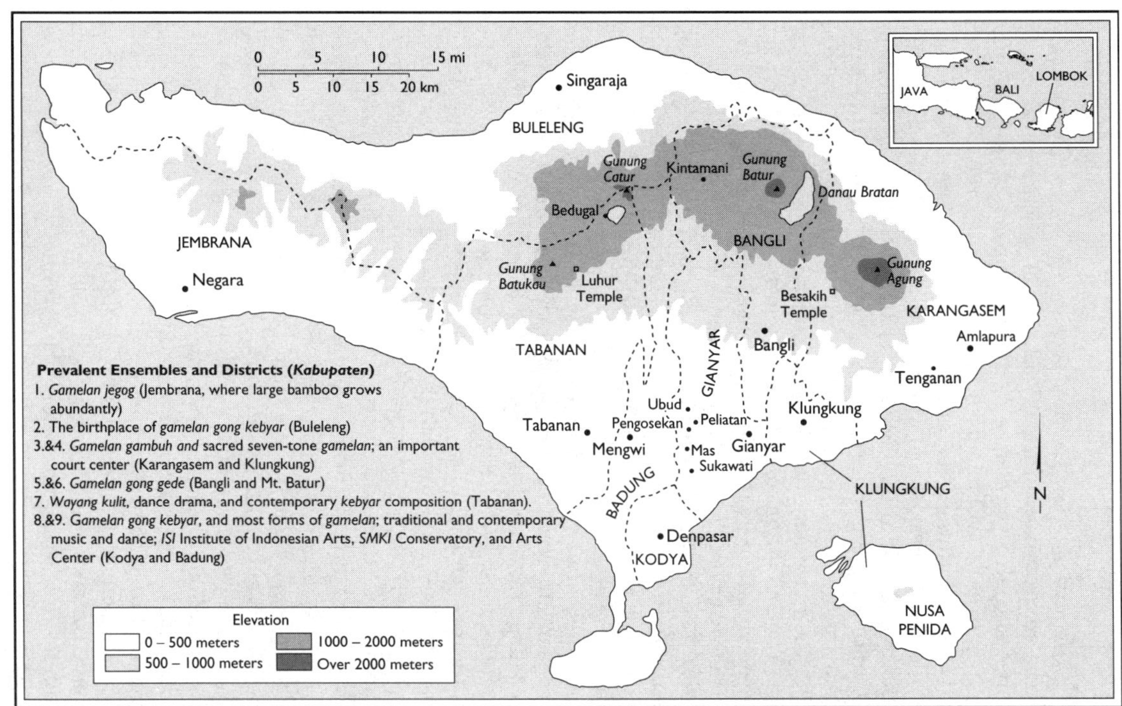

FIGURE 1.2 *Map of Bali, showing volcanoes and some important gamelan types.*

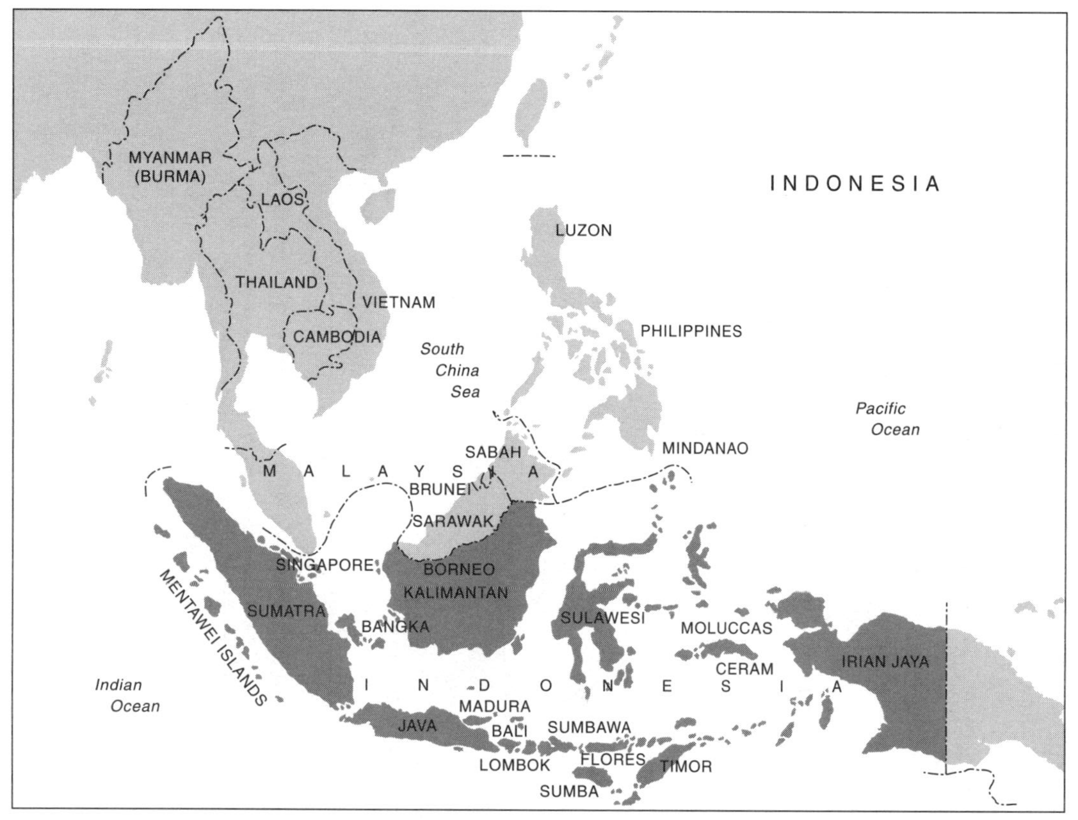

FIGURE 1.3 *Map of Indonesia showing Bali.*

mountable conditions such as deep river valleys and volcanoes and mountainous areas. Since the twentieth century this has changed for the most part, yet regional variation and pride remains. Even within each region what is the case in one village may be entirely different in an adjacent village. Musical instruments, playing styles, and versions of pieces vary greatly, as do speech patterns, dialects, and according to many Balinese, personalities and temperament. *Gamelan* types and pieces vary in function from one place to another. In this book you will learn of a select few as examples of a diverse many. Bear this in mind while learning about Balinese worldview in the next section.

Cycles of Time. Cyclicity is an underlying structural feature in many aspects of Balinese life, including aspects of musical structure. The Balinese 210-day year comprises ten simultaneous weekly calendars thought of as repeating cycles of differing lengths. Additionally, there are even larger cycles of as many as one hundred years. The coincidence of days from different calendars results in a good or undesirable day to do something, such as inaugurate a temple or honor demons, ancestors, literature, musical instruments, even tools and cars. Households have Balinese calendars to consult, but generally people retain a mental image of the complex system, partly owing to the quality ascribed to each day and the resulting confluence of days. It makes perfect sense to one Balinese colleague, for instance, that his son has musical talent because he was born on a day on which two auspicious days associated with the arts coincided from two calendars, and he would not think of planting a garden on the "wrong" day. The lunar and Gregorian calendars are also interwoven into the system, but it is the traditional Balinese calendrical system that people follow when choosing the right or wrong day to do something. Whenever anyone needs a ceremony performed, such as a wedding, toothfiling or cremation, the family goes to the local priest, who consults his calendars and chooses the appropriate day.

With reincarnation as the basic premise, the purification rites Balinese undergo throughout their lives are seen as belonging to one huge cycle of rebirth, life, death, and rebirth. A newborn child is still linked to the world of the gods until the first of a lifelong series of ceremonies that both link the child with the world of the living and purify her or him in a hierarchical sequence that extends long after death, upon becoming a deified ancestor.

Large-Scale Time: Stories and History. Another important framework for understanding being in the world is large-scale time, or *his-*

tory. The mythological, legendary, and real fuse into the way people perceive and live their lives. Stories are interwoven into daily rituals and people's sense of their own past. From early Bronze Age migrations to the present, Bali has been exposed to outside influences. With each new cultural influx, the Balinese have incorporated new elements of religious beliefs and cultural practices, synthesizing them with indigenous ones. Indian Buddhist and Hindu culture, tourism, and globalization have all contributed to Balinese culture in some way, but ancient traditions have proved resilient. While Balinese acknowledge the cumulative synthesis that is the organic, changing present of modern Bali, certain historical periods stand out as significant markers of heritage. One of my aims in this book is to show that Balinese performing arts are expressive indicators of historicity.

Balinese trace much of their cultural heritage to the neighboring island of Java, directly west of Bali. Java was the center for a succession of Hindu kingdoms in Indonesia from roughly the fifth through the fifteenth centuries, with links to its counterparts in mainland Southeast Asia. Hinduism and Buddhism were brought to Southeast Asia by religious scholars from India along the trade routes from India to China. It was customary for monarchs to appoint a Brahmana priest as advisor in order to provide a model for his subjects and to establish his own legitimacy as divine ruler. Hierarchical caste and class systems were absorbed into cooperatively based societies throughout Southeast Asia, much of which is still evident in aspects of Balinese life.

The many narratives performed in Balinese theater represent periods in history. Languages and poetic forms from each period are preserved and maintained through regular performance. Bali is often seen as a living museum of such forms as Sanskrit chant that was once prevalent in India and Javanese poetry sung in Kawi, the Old Javanese language that is rarely in use in Java. The recitation of poetry (always sung in Bali) and enactment of stories drawn from these various periods are essential components of religious rituals and secular life.

A significant legacy from India is its literature. The Indian epics *Mahabharata* and *Ramayana* have become cultural icons throughout Southeast Asia. The myriad stories are constantly enacted in many forms of theater, all of which combine music with dance or puppetry. These stories, which tell of the Hindu pantheon of gods, goddesses, demons, and humans from mythological times, still play a major role in theater traditions in Bali. In particular, people identify with characters and stories drawn from the *Mahabharata*, telling of the adventures of the five Pandawa brothers and their one hundred evil Kurawa cousins. Portrayed with human characteristics, these characters and myths are a vehicle for the expression of everyday human concerns of the Balinese. Through this vehicle, rulers have incorporated symbolic messages and performers have expressed subversive political views.

Cultural exchange between Hindu-Javanese and Balinese courts began around the ninth century and strengthened in the eleventh century (in a period known as Kediri), when the Balinese-born king Erlangga became a powerful ruler of East Java. Stories glorifying his life became central to many of the courtly dance dramas still performed today (such as *legong*; see chapter 5). In the mid-fourteenth century Bali became part of Majapahit, Java's last Hindu empire, and Balinese courts were modeled after those of Java. When Majapahit fell to the Muslim kingdom of Demak in the late fifteenth-century, many Hindu-Javanese nobility moved to Bali. The origins of many Balinese musical traditions are traced to the eastern Balinese kingdom of Gelgel (late fifteenth through eighteenth centuries), regarded as the pinnacle of Balinese arts after the fall of Majapahit. The courts supported artists, musicians, dancers, scribes, and poets versed in the art of Old Javanese poetry (Kekawin), who composed new poetry that was uniquely Balinese and preserved Javanese poetry now virtually lost in Java.

Rulers surrounded themselves with many *gamelan* ensembles that were performed at elaborate royal spectacles as an assertion of the king's power and for religious purposes. It was believed that the bronze itself was endowed with spiritual power. When sounded, this power became palpable and was magnified by the sheer spectacle of performance. Illustrated manuscripts paint a rich picture of several types of *gamelan*, each to be played in a specific part of the palace for a certain purpose. For instance, the martial processional *gamelan balaganjur* and the large, ancient *gamelan gong gede* ("*gamelan* of the great gong") were placed on either side of the palace gates to protect the royalty. The delicate *gamelan semar pagulingan* and the *gamelan gambuh* flute ensemble were played in the king's bedchamber to accompany lovemaking. Music was portrayed as sensual and heavenly. These ensembles retain some of their early associations even when played in modern contexts. The images help when we try to make sense of the plethora of ensembles performed in close proximity in today's festivals. The sense of *ramé* (boisterous and full) appears to have been a desired aesthetic for centuries. The illustrations also depict women as well as men playing musical instruments in the palace, a practice that seems to have died out during Dutch colonial times. Since the early 1980s women musicians and women's *gamelan* groups have become more prominent in the music and dance institutions and in some villages, though they are still marginalized.

After centuries of local Balinese kingdoms warring for control, the Dutch began to take hold of Bali around 1846. This culminated in two mass suicides (called Puputan, meaning "the end"), one in 1906 in Badung and another in 1908 in Klungkung, when the Balinese nobility chose to walk straight into the Dutch army's fire stabbing themselves with ritual daggars, rather than be defeated. The Balinese royal courts gradually lost control and ceased to function as patrons of the performing arts. The Dutch government assumed this role, however, and as a result, court *gamelan* were sold to villages where many *gamelan* clubs (*sekaha*) were formed and supported by local *banjars*.

Following several shifts in power, Indonesia declared its independence in 1945 and was officially recognized by the Dutch as a unified independent nation in 1949. The first ruler of the Republic of Indonesia was the Javanese president Sukarno, half-Balinese himself, who promoted Balinese culture as an idealistic model for the rest of Indonesia. His rule ended abruptly in a military coup in 1965 followed by violence in which over one hundred thousand Balinese were killed in mass killings. General Suharto assumed the presidency that lasted until 1998, promoting national development in a period known as the New Order. The role of sponsorship of the arts, formerly held by the courts and then by the Dutch, was taken on by the national Indonesian and local Balinese government in the 1960s, when two important music and dance institutions were established: ASTI (later called STSI, College of the Performing Arts), recently elevated to university status and renamed ISI (Institute of Indonesian Arts); and KOKAR conservatory, now known as SMKI (High School of the Performing Arts). Students come from throughout Bali and elsewhere in Indonesia to study at these institutions located around Denpasar, Bali's capital city, in South Bali. These schools promote and preserve the arts and sponsor research and new composition. Despite these important contributions to the arts, a by-product of these institutions has been standardization, which has led to a threatened demise of local styles. The nationally controlled curriculum exerts its influence on what is composed and performed. However, the local Balinese directors and faculty, drawn from the highest-caliber pool of performers and artists, make efforts to balance this with research, preservation, and high-level performance.

Cultural Tourism. Tourism has long played a significant role in Balinese cultural politics. Bali's intense physical beauty, along with its performing arts and exotic religious practices, caused it to become a major tourist destination, promoted by the local and national Indonesian government. As early as the colonial period the Dutch instituted a policy of preservation of Balinese culture while simultaneously opening the island to the first Western tourists, thus creating a need for such preservation. Bali's relationship to tourism began to flourish from then on. During the 1930s foreign scholars such as Margaret Mead, Gregory Bateson, Jane Belo, and Walter Spies began to study in Bali. Among them was Colin McPhee, a Canadian composer who conducted extensive music research. His encyclopedic book *Music in Bali* (1966), in which he documents and analyzes many Balinese forms of *gamelan,* is still one of the most important works on the subject.

The present generation of tourists often bemoans the loss of the "old Bali." This is not new. Even in the 1920s the first tourists to visit Bali by steamship already expressed fear of the "impending demise of its culture" (Picard 1990: 40). In particular, the small group of foreign anthropologists and artists were "persuaded that they were witnessing the swan song of a traditional culture miraculously preserved right up until then from the corrupting influences of modernity. In fact, it is as if, since the "discovery" of the island by the avant-garde of artists and anthropologists during the 1920s, the mere evocation of Bali suggested the imminent and dramatic fall from the "Garden of Eden," a state which the Balinese could not be expected to enjoy indefinitely" (Picard 1990: 40).

The impact of tourism on the performing arts is complex. While the Republic of Indonesia has commodified Balinese performing arts with cultural tourism, there is a local demand for the tourist revenue. Certain areas have weekly and daily tourist performances, and numerous musicians participate in performances in hotels for the throngs of tourists coming to this "island of paradise" (the numbers that had reached nearly 1 million foreign and domestic tourists per year have now decreased dramatically since terrorist bombings occurred in Indonesia). Pieces composed for such performances eventually are recycled back into traditional contexts.

With a hyperawareness of change and preservation, performers continue to create new works while performing the old. In some ways, people are becoming increasingly observant of tradition in the face of change. Musicians make sure to wear traditional dress when practicing *gamelan,* and to honor all the necessary deities and demons. More and more local music and dance organizations are created, reinforcing tradition.

Innovation and creativity are balanced with preservation of tradition. This contributes to an important sound ideal. Visitors to Bali may be struck by a seemingly confusing plethora of languages and sounds, old and new, in the many performing arts media performed simultaneously and in close proximity at ceremonies, but to a Balinese ear this is the expected norm in order for a ceremony to feel complete. It is important to keep in mind the value placed on completeness when studying Balinese music because it helps define a fundamental aspect of Balinese aesthetics. Not only is it important for sonic and other spaces to be filled, but references to the past must also be made.

ACTIVITY 1.1 *Three themes review*

Reviewing the three themes presented in the beginning of this chapter will help you to understand how types of gamelan *have become such important symbols for other aspects of life. Keep these themes with you as you return to the* odalan *and the concept of* desa, kala, patra.

The themes stress that: (1) community participation is highly valued; (2) music, dance, and theater are intrinsically linked; and (3) performing arts genres embody the past and present.

THINKING IN THREES: HISTORICAL PERIODS, DEGREES OF SACREDNESS, AND SPATIAL ORIENTATION OF THE PERFORMING ARTS

Although there are many periods in Balinese history, when grouping categories of performing arts genres Balinese scholars usually speak of three: Old (genres of indigenous pre-Hindu Bali, known as *Bali Aga*); Middle (showing Hindu-Javanese influence) and New (twentieth-century genres that developed out of those of the Middle category). Stories and their accompanying ensembles, repertoires, and dance styles are associated with each of the three periods.

The All-Encompassing Adat (Tradition). In traditional Balinese thought there is no distinction between sacred and secular life. These terms and concepts were imported out of necessity, to be explained below. The term *adat,* meaning "tradition," encompasses religion (for which there is now a distinct Indonesian term, *agama*), divine cosmic and social order, and all community activities. Traditionally, *gamelan* performance, dance, and other forms of creative expression are linked to function in ritual activities. Performances fit into a continuum of contexts ranging from highly sacred performances for gods to less sacred performances for gods and humans. There is a general correlation between the age of a particular story, dance, theatrical form, ensemble, or piece and its degree of sacredness. The older the form, the more sacred and unchanging it is. In *odalan* and other situations there is room and a need for all sorts of performances from old to new, thus keeping the arts relevant and vibrant.

With a rise in tourism, what had functioned as an organic, flexible system within the context of ceremonies became codified with the advent of performances held on proscenium stages for paying tourists. The issue arose that dances, in other contexts performed for gods, ought not to be traded as a commodity for money in an unconsecrated performance space. As a way of protecting the older, sacred performing arts from being exploited by tourism, in 1971 a committee of artists, religious specialists, and government officials proposed a classification system, placing music, dance, and theater genres into the three categories: *wali* (sacred), *bebali* (ceremonial), and *balih-balihan* (secular, literally, "things to be watched"). These three categories already existed to some extent, but the precise placement of genres into categories was, and is, not standardized.

Scholars have observed some problems with this simplistic distinction. One problem, for example, stems from the fact that there is no "secular" performing arts category in Bali. As the dancer and scholar I Wayan Dibia points out, even in *balih-balihan* contexts, performers still feel that they are performing for a "divine audience." "In fact, during the time of a temple ceremony the entire village is being watched by the gods" (Dibia 1992: 68), and therefore even the least sacred arts are still considered sacred to a certain extent. Furthermore, even in tourist performances performers may enter into trance states and always regard the performances with the same reverence that they would temple performances.

The distinction between *wali* and *bebali* is similarly problematic. The terms *wali* and *bebali* "have in fact as a common etymology the Sanskrit root *bali*—the very name of this island—which signifies 'offering' "(Picard 1990: 67). Although the distinction is sometimes ambiguous even to Balinese specialists, they follow this tripartite system. The system works to a certain extent because it is overlaid with fundamental Balinese attitudes toward their surroundings and worldview.

The three categories that designate relative degrees of sacredness are also linked to spatial orientation. The Balinese village, temple, and house compounds are laid out in relation to the *kaja/kelod* axis (toward the mountain or sea respectively). The proximity to *kaja* and *kelod* is relative and exists independently within each area. For instance, within a village the main temple would be located at its furthest *kaja* end while the death temple and cremation grounds would be at the *kelod* end. But in the next village to the *kelod* (south/west) *its* furthest point to the *kaja* direction would be adjacent to the point furthest *kelod* of its neighbor. A Balinese house compound consists of several covered or semi-enclosed pavilions, and enclosed structures within a walled outdoor area. The pavilions are used for ceremonial and living activities. A walled house temple within the compound would be located in the *kaja* area and the pigsty or bathroom would be located in the *kelod* area. So one pigsty might be adjacent to a neighbor's house temple. Further, spatial orientation includes the dimension of height in relation to the ground: the activities held on the ground tend to be devoted to ground spirits or demons (such as animal sacrifices or blood and liquor poured onto the earth), whereas the high Brahmana priest sits elevated on a raised pavilion where he can better communicate with the gods and deified ancestors.

The temple is composed of a series of walled courtyards, usually two or three, which set sacred space and time apart from the outside world (figure 1.4). These walls represent borders between levels of spiritual purity. A wall that prevents evil spirits from entering also surrounds every Balinese house compound.

Each of the three types of activities, including musical performance, takes place in relation to this spatial orientation, which designates its degree of sacredness and the intended audience. *Wali* activities are the most sacred, taking place in the innermost courtyard of the temple (*jeroan*), which is the furthest in the *kaja* direction, for an audience of gods who are the invited guests of the ceremony. *Wali* performances are generally integrated into religious rituals. If there is a choice available, the type of performance selected for *wali* activities would be from the Old category of the three historical periods. *Bebali* activities take place in the middle courtyard (*jaba tengah*) and are considered "ceremonial"; their intended audience includes both gods and humans. These activities are not integrated into the ritual but rather are parallel to it, and they would be chosen from the Middle period of Balinese music history. *Balih-balihan* activities are performed outside the temple or in

FIGURE 1.4 *Temple in relation to mountain.* Jaba *would be outside the temple in this case.* *(Drawing by I Dewa Putu Berata.)*

Time Period	Old (Pre-Hindu)	Middle (Hindu-Javanese Influence)	New (20th-century descendents of previous category
Degree of sacredness	*Wali* (sacred)	*Bebali* (ceremonial)	*Balih-balihan* (secular)
Audience	Gods	Gods and people	People
Placement	Inner courtyard	Middle courtyard	Outer courtyard/ outside of temple
Direction	kaja --->		*kelod*

FIGURE 1.5 *Three periods, degrees of sacredness, audience, and spatial orientation.*

an outer courtyard (*jaba*) and are intended as entertainment for humans. Nevertheless, they are performed during the temple ceremony period when the entire area is watched over by gods. These performances are generally the latest creations, or at least drawn from the New performance category. A chart of the tripartite links between historical periods, degrees of sacredness, audience, and spatial orientation is shown in figure 1.5.

Within this plan the performance spaces vary from an unmarked area on the ground to stages of various sorts. The traditional rectangular stage area, temporarily created on the ground in the middle and outer courtyards of the temple, enables the audience to be integrated into performances as they crowd around three sides, with the *gamelan* seated along the fourth. For shadow puppet performances within the temple the screen and performance area is often erected on a small pavilion in one of the courtyards. Try to keep in mind this background information as we return to the *odalan*.

In the Sacred Space of the Inner Courtyard* (Jeroan): *Old-Period Genres as Offerings. We followed the throng, stepping over narrow doorway steps, past the middle courtyard and entered the inner courtyard. After the frenetic pace of the outside I suddenly felt as though I were entering a slow-motion world. I could hear a powerful, loud, deep *gamelan* playing a long, slow composition. The air was thick with incense, through which I watched a group of women dancing with slow, fluid movements. My teacher's daughter Wayan joined them. They danced in synchronicity, yet the dance was not choreographed down to its every gesture, and each dancer moved in her own way. This is an offering dance done for the visiting gods. This type of dance has been adapted for stage and is always performed at the beginning of secular performances. In those cases the women all wear matching, elaborate costumes and perform a precise memorized choreography that is stylish and modern. A plethora of such compositions are constantly being created. But this was different. Tonight I felt as if I were witnessing people in an altered state of consciousness—the sacred quality was palpable. The women were in a different time and space from the mere here and now.

> Ngayah. *Later I asked a friend and well-known dancer, Ibu Ketut Arini Alit, whether the dance itself is considered to be an offering, and she explained that the food is the offering and dance is the way of giving it to the gods. It is a gesture of respect called* ngayah *that dancers and musicians offer selflessly in the* odalan *and say that they feel fulfilled in doing so. Ibu (the honorific title for mother or Mrs.) explained that through the combination of incense, food, beautifully colored flowers, artwork, music, and dance the gods are honored. Again, the idea of completeness should be kept in mind.*

After the dancers finished, the gamelan began to play another piece, drawn from a repertoire of pieces known as *lalambatan* (slow music) reserved for temple ceremonies. In playing this type of piece, the local *gamelan* was evoking a rare, ancient type of ensemble known as *gamelan gong gede,* formerly used for such pieces. *Gamelan gong gede* would have some forty-five members playing huge metallophones, gong-chimes, drums, and cymbals, here adapted to be played on the more contemporary smaller ensemble. The compositions in this repertoire are the longest and therefore most difficult to memorize, with slow-moving skeletal melodies played by the largest metallophones. The rows of gong-chimes play elaborating parts, providing subtle variations of the slow main melody. It is easy to understand why older pieces are fitting for the more sacred contexts—they create a mood and a time out of time. This *lalambatan* began with a metrically free introduction played by a soloist on a gong-chime instrument called *trompong* (CD track 3). The opening and brief excerpts of the lengthy main body of the piece proper can be heard in CD track 4 ("Jagul").

Mingling with this powerful bronze sound were two different types of vocal chant: specialists in the Kawi (Old Javanese) language took turns singing poetry and paraphrasing into Balinese. In the distance could be heard a thin wispy sound of many people singing *kidung*, a different form of chant sung in an old Javanese meter for ceremonial purposes. The pitches of the voices were nothing like those of the *gamelan*, and a mood of serenity was created by the melodies that seemed to fit into no other tuning system. The people singing *kidung* were squatting here and there throughout the courtyard while a low priest officiated, and the coordination of their voices was extremely loose, some following behind others who knew the melodies better.

In another corner of the courtyard a shadow puppet performance was in progress but there was no screen. It was a ceremonial form of shadow play known as *wayang lemah* (Preface Photo) and no one seemed to be watching, even though the shadow master was singing and acting out the play with great feeling. His songs and action were accompanied by the most delicate, intricate *gamelan*, known as *gamelan gender wayang* (figure 1.6). The tuning and timbre of this metallophone quar-

FIGURE 1.6 Gamelan gender wayang, *a quartet of ten-keyed metallophones with bamboo resonators that accompanies the shadow play. The sound pulsates as it wafts through the tube resonators and is played with two mallets providing a contrapuntal texture.* Gender wayang *musicians from Tunjuk, Tabanan: I Nyoman Sumandhi, Pak Sukantri, Pak Winatha, Pak Nengah.* (Photo by Lisa Gold.)

tet, quite different from that of the *gamelan gong*, has a sweet sound (CD track 5).

Shortly after the *wayang* began, the *gamelan gong* started up again, this time accompanying a masked (*topeng)* dancer who was single-handedly enacting an entire story by going behind a makeshift curtain after each dance and changing masks. He would enter the stage area with each new character, mood, and dance gestures (see chapters 4 and 5, CD tracks 6 and 7).

After Wayan finished her offering dance she joined the rest of the people seated on their knees on the ground ready to pray. On a high pavilion so that he was barely visible sat a Brahmana priest dressed in white. He was ringing a bell, performing symbolic Indian hand gestures (*mudras*) and chanting in Sanskrit. The interconnectedness of things was apparent as I moved from watching the topeng dancer's hand gestures to those of the priest (figure 1.7). Both used *mudras* from Bali's Indian past.

In the Ceremonial Space of the Middle Courtyard (Jaba Tengah): *Middle-Period Genres.* We walked out into the middle courtyard, where a *gambuh* dance drama was beginning (CD track 8). This dance drama and its *gamelan*, actually from the Middle category of Balinese music history, are considered to be one of the oldest in Bali. Though many newer forms have developed from it, the link to modern ensembles was not apparent on first glance. The ensemble consisted of four men playing four large vertical bamboo flutes, a *rebab* (bowed spiked lute), a pair of small drums, gongs, and an array of tiny bronze percussion instruments. One by one characters entered, some alone, others in groups. The dancers danced in a graceful, slow style, and women inserted inflected speech in the upper register of their voices in Kawi, a language that most of the audience could not understand. The dancers enacted tales of the Javanese prince Panji.

As my teacher's family left the middle courtyard we encountered a sudden flurry of people exiting the temple on their way to a sacred spring. Throngs of people flooded out the narrow stone gateway and down the steep steps, snaking their way through the crowds. The flurry was accentuated by drums, gongs, and cymbals, played by many individuals, each contributing to a complex interlocking texture (CD tracks 9 and 10). This processional *gamelan*, known as *balaganjur*, creates excitement to instill crowds and encourage people to march in the procession while also scaring away demons. An old Balinese manuscript describes this ensemble's martial association at the courts, also known

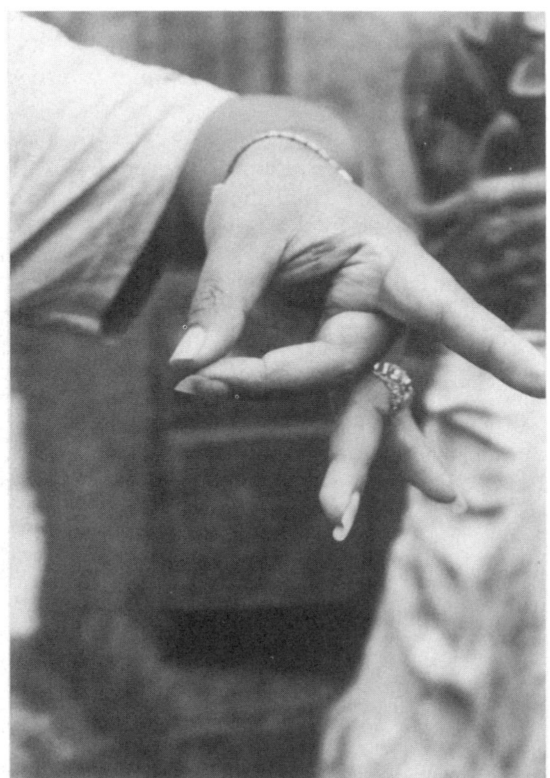

FIGURE 1.7 Topeng *dancer's hands in a mudra; I Nyoman Cerita, dancer.* (*Photo by Lisa Gold.*)

as *bebonangan* for its gong-chime kettles, which are otherwise called *bonang*: "Thus when the gamelan *bebonangan* is played, the world feels like it is shaking to the sound of thunder, and this creates fear in the mind, as if the earth feels like it is being destroyed by the sound of the bebonangan. It is the gamelan of the glorification of weapons, especially the king's state weapons, and for the warlike dance exercises of weapons in the great field [in the palace]" (*Aji Gurnita* treatise, in Vickers 1985: 165).

This association was clear as I watched another group of people exit the temple, some holding spears and other weapons, others holding a white sacred cloth many meters long that seemed to be pulling along small golden palanquins held on people's shoulders. These were little shrines where deities and ancestors were visiting, and they were being led to a spring for holy water.

The More Secular Space of the Outer Courtyard (Jaba): *New Creations and Entertainment.* After they had passed and the sound of the *balaganjur* began to fade into the distance, Wayan wanted to go to the area where a stage had been erected for a *drama gong* performance soon to begin. This is Balinese melodrama, involving music, dance, and speech. It is extremely popular. When we got there the area was totally packed with people standing to get a glimpse of the stage. Some people would remain standing to watch all night.

On the stage was a large *gamelan gong kebyar* that Wayan just called the "gong." When they began their instrumental piece preceding the drama the audience immediately cheered and applauded the sudden burst of technical virtuosity, even while the piece was still in progress. There were many such sudden musical bursts, known as *kebyar* ("explosive"), also the name for this twentieth-century flashy style of composition. It was clear that tight precision and working well as a single unit was necessary in order to produce such crisp, virtuosic, vivacious music (CD track 11).

CONCLUSION

Working together in a group to produce a composite whole enables daunting work to be accomplished and extraordinary music to be played. This is not to say that Balinese society is a communal utopia devoid of social problems and interpersonal tensions. Bali's history contains centuries of warring kingdoms and social oppression by elite minorities, followed by other kinds of political oppression and violence in the twentieth century. But the English word "stress" has only recently been adopted by Balinese who need to express a late twentieth-century phenomenon, largely a by-product of the need to keep up with the fast-paced lifestyle of the modern world. Coping strategies have been adopted, mostly from traditional values and practices that endure in the face of change. The island of Bali does not exist in a vacuum; it is very much a part of the Indonesian nation and the world at large. Yet the value people place on looking inward (in many respects, including *kaja*) supports the maintenance of a strong local cultural identity. The cherished ideals enable cooperation, group harmony, and continuity of tradition with room for individual creativity.

In this chapter the temple ceremony was situated within its web of meaning constructed by Balinese worldview. Many strands remain to be unraveled and analyzed one by one before we put them back together and stand back to view the entire image or hear all the components of a piece. In the following two chapters I bring music into focus, beginning with the ancient art of gong making and moving to instruments and their roles.

ACTIVITY 1.2 Odalan *review*

To review the variety of gamelan and theatrical genres introduced in this chapter, and also the way in which multiple performance media occur simultaneously, photocopy figure 1.5 and fill it in with indication of where and which performances occurred in the odalan *that I have described. Be sure to indicate the directions* kaja *and* kelod *on your diagram.*

Review the three themes of this volume and analyze how examples from the odalan *illustrate these themes. Write a summary that incorporates these Balinese concepts:* ramé; kaja and kelod; desa, kala, patra; *completeness;* ngayah; adat *(see Eiseman in resources).*

ACTIVITY 1.3 *Apply your analysis of the* odalan *to music in your life*

Think of some instances where music is used to shape an event in your world (eg., sporting events, raves, rock concerts, religious ceremonies). Map this in terms of spatial orientation and changes occurring over time. You may make a diagram of the spatial layout and orientation of the event as you did in Activity 1.2. How does music help a community to bond, to express individuality or group cohesion or solidarity? Does the music support changes that occur in mood and tempo? Do different genres of music symbolize different things? Are there underlying concepts that are equivalent to the Balinese ones listed in activity 1.2?

CHAPTER 2

Instruments: Materials, Tuning, and Timbre

A variety of materials can be used to make Balinese instruments resulting in quite contrasting timbres. Instruments range from struck bamboo idiophones, bamboo flutes, and blown reeds or jaw harps meant to imitate interlocking animal sounds such as frogs and crickets, to bronze ensembles of great splendor and sophistication. The most frequently used materials in *gamelan* are bronze, bamboo, hardwood, and occasionally iron. The majority of *gamelan* instruments are bronze idiophones such as gongs, gong-chimes, metallophones, and cymbals. The bronze-keyed metallophones often have bamboo tube resonators and are set in ornately carved wooden cases. Some carving has symbolic spirits such as Bhoma (a village protector, see carving of gong stand in frontispiece) and animals such as the *naga* (serpent), while others may contain scenes from the *Mahabharata* or *Ramayana* epics, finished off with gold leaf and other ornate painting. There are also membranophones played by only one or two musicians leading the ensemble (drums known as *kendang*), aerophones (vertical bamboo flutes known as *suling*) and occasionally a single type of chordophone (a bowed, spike lute known as *rebab*). This chapter introduces you to the major instrument types. Don't expect to fully understand what you listen to while reading this chapter. The next chapter demonstrates how instruments function in music. For now, just familiarize yourself with the different types of instruments and their timbres.

Ensembles consist of either bronze-keyed instruments or bamboo-keyed instruments, with the exception of some rare ancient ensembles that combine the two, or have iron or wooden-keyed instruments. Bamboo is readily available, and bamboo instruments are so easy to make that they can be heard in places where a community cannot afford a bronze *gamelan*. One often hears people casually playing on bamboo xylophones in their homes.

FIGURE 2.1 *Bamboo* gamelan jegog *xylophone, prevalent in west Bali.* (*Photo by Lisa Gold.*)

Each of the numerous types of *gamelan* has its own history and place of origin and is distinctive in its own way in terms of repertoire, materials, tuning, size, timbre, and number of instruments. Historical factors cause south central Bali to be known still for its regal and delicate bronze ensembles and dances that once were supported by the royal courts. Some *gamelan* accompany specific forms of theater, while others have a repertoire restricted to instrumental ritual accompaniment. Availability of materials causes some *gamelan* to be found only in certain regions of the island. For instance, west Bali, with its dense bamboo forests, is known for *gamelan jegog,* consisting of idiophones made entirely of bamboo from huge to small tubes that cause the earth to shake when played (figure 2.1, CD track 12).

THE POWER OF BRONZE

Balinese trace the lineage of *gamelan* to ancient bronze "kettle drums" that date back to the Dongson culture (from roughly the fourth century B.C.E. to the first century C.E.) of southern China, which spread to what is now Vietnam. The term "drum" used by scholars is a misnomer, since

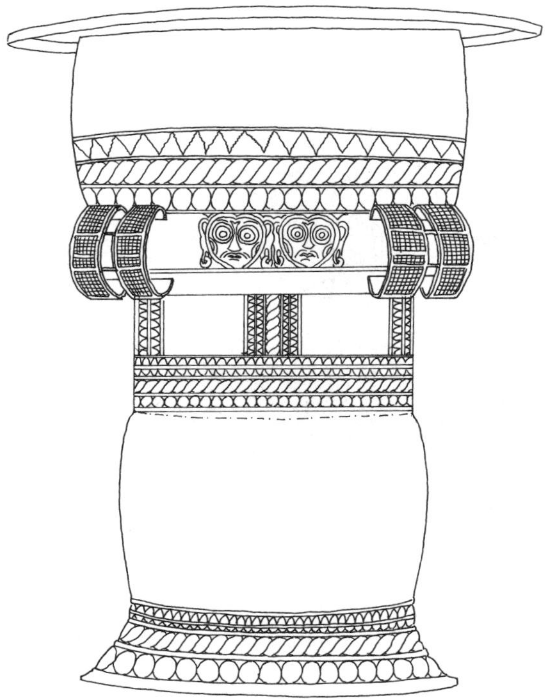

FIGURE 2.2 *The "Moon of Pejeng" bronze drum from the temple Pura Penataran Sasih (*sasih, *"moon") at Pejeng (Intaran). Its ornamentation represents early Indonesian cosmological symbolism. Believed to have been made in Bali, it is the largest of its type (186.5 cm in height). (Drawing by I Dewa Putu Berata.)*

they are not membranophones but bronze idiophones. These "bronze drums" are believed to have had great spiritual power. They were used to communicate with the spirit world for such rituals as procuring rain or healing. Bali possesses one of the most important specimens, known as the "Moon of Pejeng," named after a Balinese legend in which a wheel (the drum) of the chariot that carried the moon through the night sky became detached and fell into a tree at the village of Pejeng (figure 2.2). Whereas they are played in other parts of Southeast Asia, no bronze drums are played in Bali today, and the Moon of Pejeng is displayed lying on its side in a pavilion of the temple Pura Penataran. It is highly revered, however, for its great ritual symbolism and inherent power.

Sharing a tradition found historically throughout Southeast Asia, the possession of *gamelan* ensembles in Bali has always represented empowerment, both spiritual and otherwise. This is partly due to the inherent power believed to exist in the bronze when sounded, and to the great cost of manufacturing the metal. Kings would surround themselves with bronze ensembles to be played for state and ceremonial occasions to display their great wealth while protecting them from evil spirits or forces. This is essential in a place such as Bali where power and strength are measured by unseen forces of "inner power." Most people consult local spiritual practitioners trained in the indigenous arts of magic and healing whenever they become ill or injured.

In Bali (and Java, where gongsmithing developed) the smiths still belong to a special strata of society who undergo spiritual training that enables them to control the powerful spirits that inhabit the instruments and give them their life force. The art of bronze casting (pouring a molten blend of tin and copper into a mold to make the ancient "bronze drums") has developed into a highly sophisticated art of forging. With casting, in order to obtain the final three-dimensional shape of the large bronze kettles the top was a separate flat piece that was later attached to the base. With forging came a technique of hammering the hot bronze into the desired shape, then cooling it and repeating the process of heating and beating, thus tempering the metal. This results in an entirely different sound produced by the bronze, far more resonant and able to maintain pitch once tuned.

Watching a gong being forged is almost like witnessing a musical performance: a number of gong smiths work together so that every movement is coordinated (figure 2.3). First copper and tin are melded together to produce molten bronze, which is poured into a mold in the shape of a pancake. When hardened it is placed in a fire and hammered into the three-dimensional, bossed gong shape. One person operates the handheld bellows to fan the fire while another holds the gong with tongs and turns it to allow two other people to hammer it into shape. The hammers strike consecutively after each turn of the gong, sounding in a rhythm that recalls interlocking parts in *gamelan* music.

TUNING AND TIMBRE

All instruments in a gamelan are made and tuned together as a unique unit. One would not take an instrument from one set and play it with another set of instruments because the tuning would differ. In addition to the gongs (most large ones are ordered from gong smiths in Java),

FIGURE 2.3 *Gongsmiths making a gong in Java.* (*Photo by Benjamin Brinner.*)

the smith makes the metallophones and cymbals. It is up to the gong smith to tune the instruments. Typically, drums and flutes are made not by the gong smith but by separate specialists. Flutes are ordered to match the tuning of particular *gamelan*.

THE WAVES OF PAIRED TUNING: A *GAMELAN'S* BREATH OF LIFE

Balinese *gamelan* have a timbre often described as "pulsating" or "shimmering." This effect is achieved by "paired tuning." Each instrument in a pair of metallophones is tuned slightly apart from its partner instrument. When played together the higher instrument, known as the "inhaler" (*pengisep*), and the lower, the "exhaler" (*pengumbang*), create this pulsating effect, metaphorically breathing and thus bringing the sound of the gamelan to life. Another translation for these terms is "sucker" and "hummer"(from the word for bee), also expressing the interaction of the two pitches as a metaphor from nature. When there is more than one of a single instrument, such as in the metallophone section, the inhalers are all tuned alike and the exhalers are all tuned alike. The Balinese term for this vibrato, "wave" (*ombak),* evoking the ocean image as well as the breath, is also used to describe the pulsating reverberation of the gong. When evaluating a *gamelan,* musicians always strike the gong first to listen to the quality of its wave.

ACTIVITY 2.1 *The "waves" of paired tuning*

*On CD track 13 first you will hear a single note played on one instrument (the higher "inhaler") of a pair of metallophones (*jublag; *see figure 2.5). Then you will hear the same key struck on the "exhaler" instrument of the pair. Do you notice that it is slightly lower in pitch? Also note the smoothness of the decaying tone when each is played alone. Then listen to the two struck at the same time to hear the pulsating* waves.

Next, listen to the waves *produced by a metallophone of a higher register (the* gangsa pemade*). Each gamelan tuner aims for a specific number of pulsations per second when tuning the instruments. With some tuners, these may vary depending on the register, from low to high, while other tuners maintain that the rate of pulsating should remain throughout the registers.*

Try pairing up with a friend and see if you can replicate this with instruments that you play, such as two recorders or electric guitars.

TUNING SYSTEMS, SCALES, AND NOTATION

While there is no standardized pitch, every gong smith has his own conception about particular tuning and the intervals for each type of gamelan that fit into a recognizable system. There are tuning systems of four, five, six, and seven pitches. Most tunings are thought to be derived from two Javanese parent scales, *slendro* (a five-tone system with wide intervals) and *pelog* (a seven-tone system with wide and narrow intervals). Often gamelan tunings and vocal genres do not fit neatly into either system, and many musicians follow the Balinese practice of referring to a tuning by a type of *gamelan*, using the Balinese term *saih*, meaning "sequence of pitches." For example, one might call the tuning of *gender wayang* either *slendro* or simply *saih gender wayang.*

Other *gamelan* are tuned to scales extracted from the seven-tone *pelog* or from the five-tone *slendro*. Some older *pelog* ensembles such as *gambang, gambuh,* and *semar pagulingan,* have a seven-tone tuning, yet compositions favor five tones and thus are essentially in pentatonic modes. These older compositions are generally slow, with complex melodies that frequently *modulate* (change mode within the piece). To simplify this discussion I will call these pentatonic extractions of seven-tone *pelog* "pentatonic scales" because "mode" is a complex subject that has not been developed in any codified Balinese theoretical system. The term *mode* (implying much more than the sequence of pitches used in a piece) encompasses elements such as melodic contour, tonal center, and gong tone. (In chapter 6 I will briefly return to mode in relation to pieces played on seven-tone *gamelan*, but this will not be a focus here.) The pentatonic scales may draw on one or two of the "extra" tones (i.e., external to the mode) to "sweeten the line." In figure 2.4 the letter *P* indicates the two pitches that are external to the mode (called *pamero*). The most prevalent gamelan tuning is *selisir* (see below).

The Balinese pitch-naming system assigns each degree of the scale a syllable. Since the scales are pentatonic, there are only five pitch names in regular use: *nding, ndong, ndeng, ndung,* and *ndang* (abbr. *i o e u a*). Each syllable is notated with a Balinese symbol. This notation and solfège system was adopted at the national music conservatory in the 1960s (then KOKAR). It is sometimes called *"nding-ndong* notation," which may be helpful as a reminder that *nding* is the first degree of the scale. Activity 2.2 and figure 2.4 demonstrate the *selisir* scale along with two others, *tembung* and *sunaren*. (There are others.) Notice that the base pitch *(nding)* for each mode is on a different degree of the parent scale. By "base pitch" I do not necessarily mean "tonal center." The tonal center is determined by the pitch that the melody gravitates toward and is emphasized by the striking of a gong or by the melodic contour, and this can vary within any given mode.

parent pelog scale approximate western pitch	1 C♯	2 D ↑	3 E	4 F♯ ↑	5 G♯	6 A	7 B
Selisir-*Gong Kebyar* Tuning and Solfege	nding	ndong	ndeng	P	ndung	ndang	P
tembung	ndung	ndang	P	nding	ndong	ndeng	P
sunaren	P	ndung	ndang	P	nding	ndong	ndeng

FIGURE 2.4 KOKAR (ding-dong) *notation. P* = pamero, *pitch external to mode, a "gap" where tone is omitted, always placed between scale degrees* ndeng *and* ndung *and between* ndang *and* nding. ↑ *indicates somewhat higher pitch.*

ACTIVITY 2.2 *Three pentatonic scales in the* pelog *tuning system*

On CD track 14 a musician sings the solfège syllables for the selisir *scale. This is followed by* selisir *played on a low metallophone* (jublag), *then* tembung *and* sunaren *scales played by a full group. The numbers notated below indicate the keys of the seven-keyed metallophone: the lowest key is pitch 1. The pitches are played on metallophones with a single octave range, resulting in leaps at the point where there is no high key for the required pitch (i.e., 1 2 in* tembung *and 2 3 in* sunaren*). If you were to try to play the scales on the piano you would hear that the intervals fall in the cracks between the keys. Try singing along with the numbers and locate the scale on figure 2.4 while listening to the CD.*

Selisir	*1 2 3 5 6*
Tembung	*4 5 6 1 2*
Sunaren	*5 6 7 2 3*

These syllables originally were linked to the vowel sounds in ancient poetry that were translated into musical pitches. Although this original usage is rather esoteric, musicians today use the syllables in teaching and studying compositions. Balinese music is transmitted (taught) by rote. The teacher plays a phrase, then the students repeat the phrase until they have learned it. Then the teacher plays the phrase and continues, gradually adding phrases until the entire piece is learned. This is usually done in rehearsal of the full group rather than privately. Notation is rarely used in the transmission process and never used in performance. However, versions of the notational system known as *grantangan* are used for preservation of the skeletal pitches of long compositions. Composers sometimes refer to a notated sketch of the basic melody while teaching a group a new composition. Older pieces are preserved in palm-leaf manuscripts that have the syllables inscribed in the palm leaves.

Cipher Notation

In this book I sometimes use cipher notation (adopted from Javanese kepatihan *notation but rarely used in Bali) to make following along with examples easier. Most of the examples use the five-tone* selisir *scale. Think of extracting these from a seven-keyed metallophone as in activity 2.2 and figure 2.4. Notice that the pentatonic scales share a pattern* i-o-e—u-a, *in other words, three adjacent pitches, then a skipped pitch, then two adjacent pitches. The ciphers I use indicate this pattern of 1-2-3—5-6-. A dot over or under a number indicates a high or low octave, respectively. A dot between numbers indicates a beat in which no note is played (i.e., a* rest*). It usually means that the previous note is sustained rather than damped. To follow along with the cipher notation in this book, pat the pulse while reading the ciphers. Beginning with the gong, read across from left to right. Be sure to keep the pulse going while reading the dot rests.*

GAMELAN GONG KEBYAR: THE EXPLOSIVE TWENTIETH-CENTURY STYLE

The *gamelan* through which I will introduce Balinese instruments in this and the next chapter is *gamelan gong kebyar*. Music and ensembles are constantly being created by a process that recycles the old while creating something new. That was the case in north Bali around 1915 when a new and exciting form of gamelan and musical style was created that quickly spread throughout the island: *gamelan gong kebyar*. This ensemble is our focus, not only because it remains the most popular and ubiquitous type of gamelan at the beginning of the twenty-first century but also because it serves well as a model for demonstrating musical principles of most other ensembles.

The word *kebyar* onomatopoetically expresses "explosive," the open musical sound produced on these large, bronze ensembles when all instruments strike together (musicians will sing out "*byar!*" while flinging open their fists to describe this open, non-damped sound), as well as a type of musical passage within pieces played on the ensemble (chapter 6). *Gamelan gong kebyar* is generally called "*gamelan gong*" or more frequently simply "*gong.*" On CD track 11 you can hear a quintessential *gong kebyar* piece, "Jaya Semara," typical of the early *kebyar* style. The final section of this piece is used throughout this and the following chapter, and the entire piece is covered in chapter 6.

Gong kebyar is tuned to a pentatonic, *pelog*-derived scale called *selisir* (above). At the time of the inception of *gong kebyar* many older, seven-tone *gamelan* were melted down in order to reuse the bronze to make new, five-tone *selisir* kebyar ensembles. By eliminating two of the pitches in the scale, musicians were better able to execute complex, rapid figuration, developing a new virtuosic technique since they no longer had to leap over the "extra" keys.

Figure 2.5 shows the instruments and their names. I recommend that you memorize them, as they will be discussed throughout the book.

INSTRUMENT FAMILIES IN *GAMELAN* MUSIC

Gong kebyar consists of gongs (kettles with a raised portion in the center, in English called a *boss*), keyed instruments (*metallophones*, i.e., with keys that are struck), gong-chimes, other melody instruments, and drums and cymbals.

Several of the types of instruments in *gamelan* occur in multiple sizes in one ensemble (see below). These different sizes produce different registers from low to high, what Balinese musicians refer to as "large" and "small" respectively due to the correlation between size of the instrument and pitch (the larger the instrument, the lower the pitch). Each instrument family of similar register works together as a smaller unit within the larger ensemble.

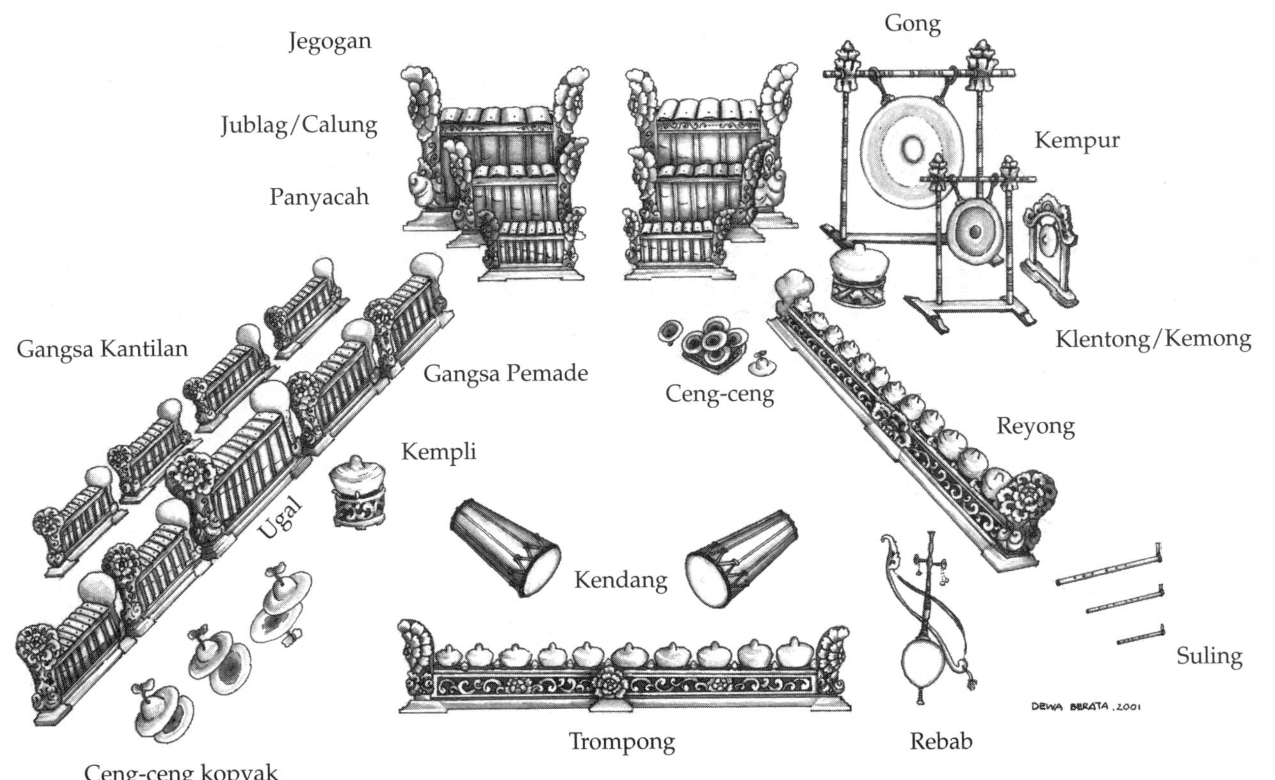

FIGURE 2.5 Gamelan gong kebyar. *(Drawing by I Dewa Putu Berata.)*

Gongs (three-dimensional, bossed circular bronze instruments; vertical = hanging):

gong	large, vertical, lowest pitch in the ensemble, soft mallet
kempur	medium-sized, vertical, pitched higher than gong, sometimes used instead of gong, soft mallet
klentong or kemong	small vertical gong, high pitched, hard mallet
kempli	horizontal, raised boss, hard mallet, plays beat

Metallophones:

The *gender* family of instruments (keys suspended over bamboo resonators)

gangsa	ten keys, hard mallet
gangsa pemade	mid-register *gangsa*
gangsa kantilan	highest-register *gangsa,* one octave higher than *pemade*
ugal	fifteen keys, hard mallet, octave lower than *pemade,* melodic leader
jublag/calung	low, five keys, soft mallet, plays the *pokok*
panyacah	low, five keys, rubber-tipped mallet, plays elaborated *pokok*
jegogan	lowest, five keys, soft mallet, plays abstraction of *pokok*

Gong-chimes (horizontal pitched gongs played as a melodic instrument):

trompong	ten horizontal gongs in a single row, one player (melodic leader), uses a pair of mallets
reyong	twelve horizontal gongs (its lowest kettle is three higher than that of *trompong*), played by four musicians, each using a pair of mallets

Non-pitched idiophones; among the various small bronze percussion are:

ceng-ceng	player holds two cymbals to strike array of several overlapping cymbals attached to a stand
ceng-ceng kopyak	pair of large hand-held crash cymbals. Several players play interlocking patterns
Drums *(kendang)*	all drums are conical with two heads and are usually played in pairs of lower (*wadon,* female) and higher (*lanang,* male) varying sizes, some hit with a mallet held in the right hand in addition to bare hands

Other melody:

suling	vertically held end-blown bamboo flute (pronounced *soo-ling*)
rebab	two-stringed, bowed spike lute of Java and Bali (pronounced *r'bahb*) played in *gambuh* and *semar pagulingan*

FIGURE 2.6 *Glossary of Balinese Instruments (and mallets) in* Gamelan Gong Kebyar

pitch ciphers	1̤	2̤	3̤	5̤	6̤	1̣	2̣	3̣	5̣	6̣	1	2	3	5	6	1̇	2̇	3̇	5̇	6̇	1̈
trompong					■	■	■	■	■	■	■	■	■	■							
reyong								■	■	■	■	■	■	■	■	■	■	■	■		
ugal		■	■	■	■	■	■	■	■	■	■										
gangsa pemade							■	■	■	■	■	■	■	■	■	■					
gangsa kantilan												■	■	■	■	■	■	■	■	■	■
jegogan	■	■	■	■	■																
jublag/calung						■	■	■	■	■											
penyacah											■	■	■	■	■						

FIGURE 2.7 *Instrument ranges and registers in* gamelan gong kebyar
1 = nding, 2 = ndong, 3 = ndeng, 5 = ndung, 6 = ndang
Balinese musicians occasionally use the ciphers 1 2 3 4 5 (although is it extremely rare that ciphers are used at all, and never in performance). I use the Javanese system of 1 2 3 5 6 because it is more widely understood and makes sense when discussing the seven-tone system from which selisir is derived.

Figure 2.7 shows the entire pitch range of a *gamelan gong kebyar*. Gong pitches are not noted here because they tend to be variable (see below). However, from the largest gong through to the highest *kantilan gangsa* the ensemble spans five octaves. The chart shows the overlap in instrument ranges.

Bronze instruments fall into two broad types: gongs and keyed instruments. Gongs provide a metric framework. A group of low-pitched metallophones plays a slow-moving basic melody and its variants. Higher pitched metallophones and gong-chimes play elaborating parts that embellish the basic melody. Thus there are many simultaneous melodies of equal prominence.

The Gongs. Gongs come in several sizes. The largest (the *gong ageng* or *gong gedé* meaning "large," hereafter referred to as *gong*) is by far the most important instrument in any *gamelan*. It is the deepest, the most resonant, and the most spiritually charged. Special offerings are always given to the spirit of the gong before any performance, and it is the gong that is said to give the particular set of instruments that comprise a *gamelan* its unique sound. The gong is not damped after it is struck, and the acoustic undulation of its decay is extremely powerful, able to penetrate the dense texture of the ensemble and to waft for miles over rice fields. Despite the variations in pitch, the largest gong always provides sonic support because of its low register and powerful timbre. Its spectral overtones are able to emphasize more than one "gong tone" as a tonal center, since melodies may be centered around any pitch in the scale. Some sets of instruments have two large gongs. As is the case with many instrument types, the larger of the pair (lower in pitch) is considered female (*wadon*); the smaller (higher) is the male (*lanang*). The lower (female) gong is usually about one octave lower than pitch 1 on the *jegogan*. The higher (male) gong is variable, pitched about a third to a fifth higher.

A medium-sized gong (the *kempur*) has similar qualities to the gong but is higher in pitch. The *kempur* is about an octave plus a fifth higher than the low gong. Like the gong, the *kempur* is struck with a padded mallet and thus is able to provide tonal support for the music. A much smaller gong, higher in pitch (the *klentong* or *kemong*), is struck with a harder mallet, thus producing a sharp attack rather than a smooth support. It is often tuned outside the tuning of the ensemble, in the upper range of the *panyacah* metallophones.

Finally, there is a horizontal gong (*kempli*) held in the player's lap or on a stand. *Kempli* pitches vary but are in the range of the *jublag*. Struck with a hard mallet, *kempli* functions as the beat keeper of the ensemble. Its part consists of evenly spaced beats that cut through the musical texture. Its tone is not sustained like that of the other three gongs because the player mutes the sound. Acting as a flexible metronome, the *kempli* player must be sensitive to constant tempo changes and able to understand and follow the complex drum part. Another such timekeeper is called the *kajar*. It is higher in pitch, has a flat boss, and can be struck on the boss or rim to produce closed or open strokes that replicate drum patterns.

ACTIVITY 2.3 *Listening to the gongs*

As you listen to CD track 15, locate each gong on figure 2.5 as it is announced.

00:00 gong wadon *(female, lower-pitched hanging gong)*

00:10 gong lanang *(male, higher-pitched hanging gong, not pictured in figure 2.5)*
00:24 kempur *(medium-sized hanging gong)*
00:31 klentong *(small hanging gong)*
00:40 kempli *(small horizontal gong, time keeper; see figure 3.4)*
00:47 kajar *(smaller horizontal gong, time keeper, plays beat or drum pattern with closed and open strokes)*

Cycles of Time in Music: Gongs that Mark Colotomic Meters. Gongs provide a structural framework for the music by repeating a regular pattern in a repeating melodic cycle. The size (hence tone and timbre) and placement of the gong give it its relative degree of emphasis. The gong framework is an extremely important reference for musicians: they always know where a part fits in relation to the gong pattern. The pattern and number of beats in the cycle tells them a lot about the form of the piece. There is no single Balinese term for this type of structure; instead, each gong form is given a name (chapter 5). The Western term *colotomic structure* (from the Greek for "divide") is often used by non-Balinese to refer to these cyclic forms. I am adopting Tenzer's term "colotomic meter" (2000) because it encompasses more than simply the gong pattern, and I avoid using the term "colotomic form" because I am reserving *form* to describe the large-scale form of entire compositions that contain these cyclic repetitions (chapter 6). I highlight my definition here for easy reference:

> I use *colotomic meter* to denote cyclic metric structures of various lengths, marked by a pattern played on gongs of various sizes and associated with specific moods, dramatic situations, genres, and drum patterns. The largest gong marks the most important stress in the music: the beginning and end of the melodic and metric cycle (which are one and the same). The *kempur* and *klentong* divide the cycle at various points depending on its structure.

In chapter 5 you will learn some colotomic meters and how they are used, but the simple sixteen-beat pattern in activity 2.4 will demonstrate the concept.

ACTIVITY 2.4 *The structural framework of gongs*

Familiarize yourself with the onomatopoetic syllables with which musicians vocalize the gong strokes. The kempli *provides a continuous beat (say* "tuk tuk tuk tuk . . . " *as in* "took"*) sixteen times per gong. The gong marks the heaviest stress on beat 16 (say* gong *or* sir, *as in* "sear"*); the* klentong *(smallest gong) strikes halfway through the cycle (say* tong*); the* kempur *(medium-sized gong) strikes before and after the tong (say* "pur" *as in* "poor"*).*

To follow along easily to CD track 16 say the pattern before playing the example, beginning on beat 16. The pattern is played twice in the first 00:21 of the track. It might be helpful to think of this pattern drawn as a repeating circle, with gong *at 12 o'clock,* tong *at 6 o'clock, and the* purs *at 3 and 9 o'clock.*

gongs:				pur				tong				pur				gong
	tuk	tuk	tuk	tuk	tuk	tuk	tuk	tuk	tuk	tuk	tuk	tuk	tuk	tuk	tuk	tuk
Beats:	1	2	3	4	5	6	7	8	9	10	11	12	13	14	15	16

Keyed Instruments (Metallophones). There are two main types of construction for metallophones. One belongs to a family called *gender* (pronounced with a hard *g*) in which the keys are strung together and suspended over bamboo resonators. Figure 2.5 shows a number of these in *gong kebyar*. The precise number varies depending on the *gamelan*, but since they work together in pairs there is always an even number of them. The other type, seen in gong gedé not in gong kebyar, is called *jongkok* ("squatting") because the keys, attached on posts inserted through holes, sit directly on the case. The two types produce quite distinct timbres: in the *gender* type the air reverberating through the bamboo tubes reinforces the vibrations of the bronze, producing a rich, windlike sound (figure 2.8), while the *jongkok* type have a sharper attack.

The keys on all metallophones must be damped after striking, otherwise the sounds would all blur together. This is done with the thumb and forefinger of the left hand, which follows the right hand after striking the key with the mallet. A variety of damping techniques produce a range from sharp to smooth articulation.

FIGURE 2.8 Jegogan *without keys, showing bamboo resonators* (gender *type construction).* *(Photo by Lisa Gold.)*

Gender-*Type Metallophones.* The metallophones in figure 2.5 are the *gender* type. They appear in several sizes but are broadly distinguished into two groups: (1) instruments of the low register (which I will call "the low instruments"), which play a basic fundamental melody, and (2) the elaborating instruments, known as the *gangsa* section. The lower the instrument, the slower-moving is the part. In the center of figure 2.5 are three sizes of low instruments. On the left side is the *gangsa* family of elaborating instruments. The leader of the metallophone section plays a larger-size *gangsa* located in the center of the other *gangsas*. The player sits up high on a stool to be visible to all musicians (figures 2.9 and 3.4).

The Low Metallophones. All the low metallophone instruments have a restricted range of a single octave (consisting of five keys, which I am numbering 1 2 3 5 6, heard in CD track 14). Notice the diagonal lines on the bamboo resonators of all the metallophones in figure 2.5 (also visible in figure 2.8), showing the nodes in the bamboo that indicate the length of each tube: the lower the note, the longer the tube. The lowest in pitch is a pair of *jegogan*. The long resonating tubes require the player to sit up high on a chair or stool. The player strikes the keys with a

FIGURE 2.9 *Women's* gong kebyar *ensemble* Puspa Sari, *with Ni Ketut Arini Alit playing* ugal. *Also featured are Desak Made Suarti playing* kendang, *Nyoman Sutiari and Lisa Gold playing* gangsa, *and other members of one of the first women's* gamelan, *founded in 1981 by I Wayan Suweca and his sister, Ni Ketut Suryatini. Women's groups began then and have become popular. Many villages have women's* gamelan, *and they participate regularly in the annual Bali Arts Festival. In 2001 for the first time mixed groups of men and women musicians entered in the* gamelan *competition at the Arts Festival, marking an important change in the way women musicians are considered. Most groups, however, are all-male ensembles.*

padded mallet. One octave higher are a pair of *jublag* that are struck by rubber-tipped wooden mallets, giving them a slightly harder attack. One octave above these are a pair of *panyacah* (pronounced *panyacha*), struck with even harder, lighter mallets. These three pairs of low-pitched instruments provide the melodic foundation on which pieces are built; their role is discussed in the next chapter, but you may hear them now in CD track 16 (see activity 3.1).

The Gangsa *Family.* The *gangsa,* another family of *gender*-type metallophones, plays elaborating melodic parts. *Gangsa* come in two sizes, the *pemade,* one octave higher than the *panyacah,* and the *kantilan,* one octave higher than the *pemade* (figure 2.5). Both have a two-octave range on ten keys and are struck with hard wooden mallets, giving them a crisp attack. In most sets of instruments all metallophones have beveled keys that enable the mallet to bounce quickly from one key to the next as musicians execute incredibly rapid figuration in the elaborating parts. The damping techniques used in playing the *gangsa* are much more demanding than those of the slower-moving parts. The *gangsa* section is led by the *ugal* player on a metallophone lower in pitch than the *pemade.* The *ugal* is larger and also has a two-octave range. Listen to CD tracks 18–24, which demonstrate the *gangsas* in isolation, for now just to hear their timbre. Activities in chapter 3 will guide you through these.

Gong-Chimes. Unlike the hanging gongs discussed above, gong-chimes are melody instruments. They are gongs that are arranged in graduated sizes and pitch from low to high (from left to right) sitting horizontally on suspended ropes in a frame. Seeing these kettles immediately makes clear why Balinese musicians refer to pitch not in terms of "low" and "high" but in terms of "large" and "small" (the larger the kettle, the lower the pitch). While the two types of gong-chimes in *gong kebyar* both embellish the fundamental melody, they have quite differing functions and playing styles.

Reyong. The *reyong* has twelve kettles and is played by four musicians (figures 2.5 and 2.10). Each player uses two mallets. Wooden sticks wrapped with string at one end, the wooden tips exposed, enable two distinct timbres: the padded sound of the string striking the boss, and the sharp attack of the wood striking the rim of the kettle. The two players on either end have four kettles on which to play, while the two inner players use two to three. Three techniques are used, two that play interlocking melodic elaboration on the boss and one that plays a percussive accentuation on the boss and the rim. Listening to CD tracks 25–28 will acquaint you with the sound of the *reyong,* but I will guide you through them in the next chapter.

Trompong. The other gong-chime instrument, the *trompong,* has ten kettles (figures 2.5 and 2.11). Its lowest kettle is three lower than that of the *reyong. Trompong* is used only in certain types of pieces that are in the minority in the *gong kebyar* repertoire. A soloist plays free-metered introductory sections and has a melodic leadership role. One of the most highly competent members of the group, he or she embellishes the basic melody somewhat freely within specific conventions (CD tracks 3,

FIGURE 2.10 Reyong *players from Sanggar Çudamani (I Dewa Putu Berata on left).* *(Photo by Lisa Gold.)*

4, and 38). Unlike *reyong*, the *trompong* does not have a non-melodic percussive function.

Other Layers of Melody. Only two instruments allow the musician to alter the pitch: the *suling* (bamboo end-blown flute) and *rebab* (two-stringed spike lute, figure 2.5). These two show clear connections with Bali's Javanese ancestry (as do many of the bronze instruments), but the playing techniques have diverged from those of their Javanese counterparts over the centuries. One reason is that the ensemble blend differs dramatically between *gamelan* of Java and Bali. *Rebab* is mainly played in older, more delicate ensembles, but occasionally in atmospheric moments in new *kebyar* compositions. In these cases it is sometimes used to play pitches outside of the pentatonic tuning. It has no frets and the strings do not touch the neck, so the musician can produce any pitch by pressing down, bending the string, or sliding up or down the neck.

A group of *suling* players elaborate with a lyrical melody, using paired tuning and a circular breathing technique to produce a constant tone. The player breathes in through his nose and stores the air in his

FIGURE 2.11 Trompong *player (I Dewa Ketut Alit, composer and member of* Sanggar *Çudamani).* *(Photo by Lisa Gold.)*

cheeks while blowing air into the instrument, often producing a wide vibrato and a constant, strong tone. Sometimes there are ornate solo *suling* passages, rhythmically free against a rigid grid provided by the gongs (CD track 30, chapter 5).

Drums: Aural Conductor of the Ensemble. Typical of *gong kebyar* is a pair of conical shaped, double-headed drums, each played by a single player (figures 2.5 and 2.12). The heads of the drums are tuned by tightening rawhide lacing running lengthwise: on each drum the left head is smaller (higher-pitched) than the right head. The tuned nature of the drum permits two drummers to play complementary patterns that interlock, forming one composite part. The lower-pitched strokes (i.e., played on the right head with the player's right hand) are generally more important to the interlocking patterns, but the higher-pitched left-hand strokes, sometimes combined with a right-hand stroke, are essential for sudden cues. One drum (the *lanang*, or the male), is slightly smaller than the other. The larger and hence lower-pitched drum is the *wadon*, or female (around 2 cm larger than the male).

The drum is the ultimate leader of the ensemble, playing special patterns to cue most musical responses. The *wadon* player is usually the

FIGURE 2.12 *Two* kendang *(drum) players using mallets.* Lanang *(male drum, played by I Dewa Putu Rai) on left,* wadon *(female drum) on right. Drums are played mostly with the hands, but sometimes with a mallet in the right hand.* Ceng-ceng kopyak *players are seated behind them (seated* balaganjur*). (Photo by Lisa Gold.)*

leader of the ensemble. Drum patterns are linked to gong structures. Repeating patterns are recognizable while flexible enough to allow for personal expression and variation. Some genres require drumming with a mallet held in the player's right hand, striking on the lower head. This is typical of *lalambatan* and *balaganjur* and some dance drumming. Otherwise, the drummer strikes with his hands.

Mnemonic syllables are used for each drum stroke when patterns are learned or conveyed. Thus a drummer is able to sing the drum pattern. The main sounds in the interlocking patterns are those produced by striking the larger (hence lower) head with the right hand. On the larger, female drum, this is *dag*, on the higher, male, this is *tut*. Many timbres can be produced, depending on the precise angle and placement of the hand on the head, on what part of the hand is used, and on whether or not the opposite head is damped while striking. Each nuance can have its own syllable. Furthermore, female and male drums have their own set of syllables so they can be differentiated when singing a composite pattern.

ACTIVITY 2.5 *Drums*

On CD track 17 you will hear the following strokes played separately, then together. First repeat each syllable after you hear it.

wadon *(female drum)*
kap *(left hand, high head, damped slap)*
kum *(right hand, struck with thumb)*
de *(right hand, open)*
lanang *(male drum)*
pek *(left hand, high head, damped slap)*
pung *(right hand, open so that it rings)*
tut *(right hand, damped)*

Next a composite pattern is recited using the mnemonic syllables. Try to repeat this before you listen to the two drummers play the pattern:

Kap pek kap pek kum pung kum pung
Kap pek kum pung de tut kum pung

At 00:23 the drum "solo" (two interlocking drums) from "Jaya Semara" *is played to give you a sense of the complexity of the interlocking patterns.*

Cymbals **(Ceng-Ceng).** Working closely with the drums is the *ceng-ceng* (set of cymbals, pronounced *cheng-cheng*). There are two main types (figure 2.5). The first consists of small, delicate, overlapping cymbals attached facing upward to a wooden stand. The player holds a small cymbal in each hand, which he strikes against the overlapping plate of cymbals. The stands usually are carved ornately to resemble symbolic animals such as the all-important turtle on which the island of Bali (i.e., the world) is believed to rest, according to Balinese mythology. This type of *ceng-ceng* is closely coordinated with the drum part and the nonmelodic *reyong* part, articulating dance movements and other important rhythmic activity (CD track 26). The other type is called *ceng-ceng kopyak* and consists of two large, hand-held crash cymbals played by pairs of musicians playing interlocking parts. They produce a loud crashing sound and are usually played in marching *gamelan bal-aganjur* (figures 2.5 and 2.12, CD tracks 9 and 10), and in *gong gede* temple pieces (CD tracks 2 and 4).

CONCLUSION

In this chapter I have introduced only a fraction of the instruments Bali has to offer. The inventiveness is astounding when considering the vast numbers of distinctly different instruments (see McPhee 1966, Tenzer 1991 and 2000, Harnish 1998, and Gold 2000). In the next chapter you will learn about the roles of the instruments and players within the *kebyar* ensemble. Imagine, if you will, walking into your teacher's home for your first *gamelan* lesson.

CHAPTER 3

Interlocking and Layering: Musical Roles in the Ensemble

Peliatan Village, 1981: *The rainy season this year has lasted for six months. Yesterday the rain was beating down so hard I was drenched the instant I stepped off my porch. People were using large banana tree leaves as umbrellas. I did not want to miss a lesson with my drum teacher, Pak I Made Lebah. He was already quite old (in his seventies) but always full of energy to teach, to drum magnificently all night in a performance, and ride his bicycle home in the morning! After getting my sandals stuck in the deep mud several times on the way, I finally arrived at his house. His granddaughter, my good friend and a well-known dancer, greeted me to say the lesson had been canceled because of the rain. Pekak (grandfather, as we called him) was asleep.*

Today the sun is shining and Pekak sits cross-legged on a pavilion in a sarong. Smiling, he explains, "If it is raining, then the lesson is off." A metallophone and a pair of medium-sized drums sit poised on the pavilion (one of the several small, raised, roofed platforms that comprise living and ceremonial spaces within a house compound, hereafter referred to as balé*). Holding one of the drums, he hums the melodic introduction to the piece we are working on,* "Legong Keraton," *cueing me to play my drum part, which dovetails into his complementary part. Over and over he plays a phrase, and I mimic him until I play it correctly. He continues on to the next phrase until we reach the end of the cycle and repeat the entire section.*

When I work on a metallophone part he follows the same process. Sitting across from me he plays everything from the reverse side of the instrument on which I play (i.e., backward), working phrase by phrase until I can play the entire piece. Then he adds the complementary part that fits in between the notes of my part. At the least mistake he stops and patiently starts at the beginning so that I get it right. This is how people are able to memorize numerous pieces of all lengths and to retain them for good. Playing interlocking parts on a single instrument at a rapid tempo is exhilarating because both players fuse into a single player. You do not think about your isolated part anymore; rather, the composite melody of both parts runs through you and your hands just seem to know how to fit in implicitly, mallet flying over keys.

When I cannot absorb any more material we stop and drink fragrant jasmine tea and eat boiled bananas (called in Balinese biu-biu malab-blab, *so wonderfully onomatopoetic) while Pekak tells me stories. He tells me about what it was like when he was Colin McPhee's "driver" in the 1930s, introducing him to musicians and* gamelan *ensembles and teaching the children's group that McPhee organized. Pekak was obviously much more than a driver; he was a guide to McPhee in every sense of the word, especially to Balinese music. He tells about coming to the United States in the 1950s with the famous Peliatan* gamelan *in which he was the drummer, or tells* wayang *stories, or shares gossip and asks me about life in America. Then we continue the lesson. Sometimes this lasts all day, with other musicians dropping by and joining in. His stories are an oral history of change in Bali throughout the twentieth century.*

The generosity of spirit and the love of sharing music, stories, and knowledge are overwhelming in Bali. Immersion in this form of pedagogy makes clear the effectiveness of oral transmission in this culture where orality and literacy merge. My teachers are repositories of vast bodies of knowledge (including memorized ancient texts along with orally transmitted knowledge of all kinds), which they generously lavish on their students.

At night I might go watch the tourist performance that Pekak and his granddaughter perform in, or join in a gamelan *rehearsal of a young group Pekak is coaching. These musicians range in age from eight years old to their early twenties. They play as seasoned adults, replete with technical virtuosity and sensitive affect. It is obvious that hearing the music since birth has had its effect on the way they have learned the music. When Pekak teaches a new piece, they clearly are absorbing new melodies as larger patterns made up of smaller components that are already familiar to them from having internalized the musical language and syntax. What is striking is not only the level of intense focus combined with joviality but also their deference to the teacher and self-confidence.*

THE MUSICAL COMMUNITY OF A *GAMELAN SEKAHA*

As noted in theme 1 of this book, people in Bali highly value community spirit and do not do things alone, but join together for all activities. The Balinese expression "*suka duka*" (happy together, sad together) is often used to describe the spirit of interaction in all sorts of community organizations. Known as *sekaha,* these organizations exist for rice cultivation, neighborhood decision making, religious ceremonies, and music making, for instance. When need arises within a community the required *sekaha* spring into action, temporarily putting aside other daily activities to work on preparations for such occasions as cremations, temple ceremonies and life cycle rites.

It is therefore not surprising that music making in Bali is almost always done in groups. Some musicians describe the various musical roles within the ensemble as being parallel to social roles of individuals within the community. One of the most salient aspects of *gamelan* is its layered texture. The listener's focus of attention may shift from one layer to another or take in the totality of the texture. This chapter guides you through the layers of sound.

The ultimate goal for any musician is to contribute to a sense of oneness with a group of musicians, whether the group is a duo or a forty-five-member ensemble. This oneness results from years of training and practicing together, working toward the ultimate aesthetic of tight precision, what some performers call "*kompak*" (compact) or "*sip*" (tight). Even though some members of any ensemble clearly play leadership roles and show greater proficiency than others, these qualities are never displayed prominently; rather, they contribute to enhancing the overall sound of the group. The way individual musicians contribute to this is analogous to the way the *gamelan* groups fit into the larger society.

When a music ensemble is good, the community feels regional pride because the very identity of a place is strongly connected to its *gamelan*; this perpetuates the desire for musicians to excel. Having music as a requirement for ceremonies helps to perpetuate creativity and stimulate musical activity. The pieces that are required contribute to shaping the mood and progression of a ceremony, much as they do in theatrical performances. The musicians are at once accompanists and participants in the ritual. As long as the required piece is being played at the appropriate time, the ceremony may be enacted. This can be done with minimal competence level, but there is room for high-level musicianship encompassing creativity that transcends that of the merely required repertoire and versions of pieces. Individual composers often train *gamelan* groups, adding their own musical flair, and the spirit of competition between groups is high.

THE STRATIFIED TEXTURE OF *GAMELAN*: SIMULTANEOUS MELODIES

The Balinese ideal of communal cooperation is beautifully exemplified in the way the various parts work together in the ensemble. The musical texture (the relationship between the parts of the ensemble) in Balinese *gamelan* is a combination of "stratified polyphony" and "heterophony." The first term refers to the layering of melodic lines that move at different rates produced by various instrument groups or "families" in different registers. The general rule is that instruments of the lower registers move at a slower rate than those of the higher registers. The second term refers to the simultaneous sounding of variants of a melody (see Wade, *Thinking Musically*). The relationship between the flutes and *rebab* can be described as heterophonic, for instance.

Please bear in mind that many equally important and simultaneous melodies are played at once. Some layers of melody really stand out in the foreground of the texture and are quite hummable, with rhythmic integrity, while others play supportive, polyrhythmic elaborating, or abstract roles. The following discussion presents instruments in the context of musical texture and function.

The Pokok *(Basic Melody).* In chapter 2 I introduced the "low instrument" group of metallophones that play a slow-moving melodic foundation. This foundation consists of repeating melodic cycles and their variants. Rather than providing something equivalent to a bass line, the low instruments are considered to be playing fundamental melodies from which the others are derived. Many simultaneous versions of the melody are played at once by the instruments of the higher registers as a form of elaboration of the lower melodies. Therefore, the entire texture consists of simultaneous melodies, all based on and derived from the same melodic idea.

Pokok (literally, "basis") is the important Balinese term used to refer to the fundamental melody and its variants. By variants I mean this: of the three pairs of low instruments, the *jublag* plays the *pokok* (basic melody) while the *jegogan* plays every two, four, or eight of the *pokok* tones. The *panyacah* may fill in the *pokok* with ornamental passing tones (see activity 3.1). The *pokok* often moves relatively slowly in evenly spaced beats.

ACTIVITY 3.1 *Basic melodies on low instruments*

Review: *Before doing this activity, review the* selisir *scale in Activity 2.2 and sing along, using the ciphers 1 2 3 5 6.*

On CD track 16 you will hear an eight-beat melody from the kebyar *piece* "Jaya Semara." *This simple, scalewise descending melody consisting of four pitches will be used for most of the examples in this chapter. Although the instruments are introduced in order from lowest to highest, it will help you to familiarize yourself with the* jublag *melody first. Try singing along with the recording by beginning on the fourth note (pitch 2) at 0:32. Get used to reading the cipher notation beginning on the last note. So if you see .1 . 6 . 3 . 2 you should begin with the 2 at the gong stroke, then read from left to right as usual. You will hear:*

2 [:.1 . 6 . 3 . 2:]

Because the melody is eight beats long (count the kempli *beats), it takes two repetitions to cover one sixteen-beat gong cycle. Review activity 2.4 and track the gong pattern as you sing.*

gongs:				*pur*				*tong*				*pur*				*Gong*
	tuk	*tuk*	*tuk*	*tuk*	*tuk*	*tuk*	*tuk*	*tuk*	*tuk*	*tuk*	*tuk*	*tuk*	*tuk*	*tuk*	*tuk*	*tuk*
pokok	.	1	.	6	.	3	.	2	.	1	.	6	.	3	.	2

Due to the limitation of a single octave, it is often necessary to leap octaves (this is called octave displacement*). In other words, when this four-tone melody is played on a multi-octave metallophone, such as it is on* gangsa *and* ugal, *the melody descends from pitch 2 to low 6̣ then jumps up to 3:*

. 1 . 6̣ . 3 . 2

When this is done, the 3 becomes the highest pitch of the phrase.

The dot under the 6 indicates a low register. A dot between notes represents an empty beat in which the note is sustained.

At 00:21 the two largest and lowest metallophones (jegogan) *enter first, playing a skeletal abstraction of the* jublag *part that articulates the main stress pitches:*

. . . 6̤ . . . 2̤

At 00:52–1:11 the two panyacah, *pitched one octave above the* jublag *and following its entrance, fill in the* pokok:

6 1 5 6 2 3 1 2

Notice how easy it is to hear the octave displacement in the panyacah *part as it leaps up from pitch 1 and approaches 6 from 5. This part gives a sense of one level of "filling in" and elaborating a simple melody.*

The melodic stress falls on the final beat of the melodic grouping rather than on the first beat. In Balinese music it is important to hear the phrasing of the melody as leading *toward* its final note, which is often marked by an instrument of lower pitch such as the gong, or in this case, by the lowest of the metallophones, the *jegogan*. In this way the beat is stressed without any added volume. The added timbral support of a low instrument such as the gong, along with its placement in the musical phrase (i.e., at the end of a grouping of notes), establishes musical emphasis and the sense of where a musical line is centered and going.

ACTIVITY 3.2 *Stress on ends of phrases*

Listen again to CD track 16 to 1:11 to feel stress on the end of the note grouping (pitch 2). Before playing the example practice counting toward the final note by saying 4-3-2-1 4-3-2-1, with emphasis on the 1. When you listen to the example try to emphasize this final note in every grouping of four by clapping, patting, or pretending to play the gong parts. You can do this with any of the three density levels. To prepare, read through each part simply as numbers and emphasize the final note in each grouping. You can then follow along with this "score" of all three parts to see how they line up. If you get lost listen for the gongs.

key: gong O *kempur* ˘ *klentong* ¯

jublag	.	1	.	6̆	.	3	.	2̄	.	1	.	6̆	.	3	.	②
jegogan	.	.	.	6	.	.	.	2	.	.	.	6	.	.	.	②
panyacah	6	1	5	6	2	3	1	2	6	1	5	6	2	3	1	②

***Communal Elaboration: Filling in all Sonic Space with Interlocking Parts* (Kotekan).** Just as the Balinese night's soundscape is filled with a multitude of sounds, in all Balinese art forms, it seems, the aesthetic ideal is fullness (*ramé*, chapter 1), intricacy, and curvaceous elaboration. This is also the case with musical texture. *Kotekan* is a communal way of playing an elaborating part, where musicians rely on a partner to complete the composite melody.

Building up from the *pokok* are two main groups of instruments that play interlocking figuration: the *reyong* and the *gangsa*. I have heard musicians explain the origin of the interlocking elaborating parts as being the sound of frogs in the evening, each with its own rhythmic pattern that seems to dovetail into those of other frogs. Others have explained it as coming from bamboo rice-pounding tubes. When a group of people pound rice together to remove the hull they often do so by alternating striking so that their rhythms fit together into a composite pattern. This has developed into an art form in its own right, practiced in west Bali (where thick bamboo grows) by women who stamp bamboo tubes against a wooden plank, playing interlocking rhythmic patterns. In this case, the origin of the art form has gone full circle, from rice pounding to *gamelan* and back to bamboo stomping tubes.

Gangsa Kotekan: Polos *and* Sangsih. The *gangsa* interlocking figuration (*kotekan*) consists of two complementary parts: the *polos* ("basic," main part), which usually plays on the beat, and the *sangsih* ("differing"), which fits into the spaces between *polos* notes. The composite melody has a faster tempo than any single player could execute alone. It is usually four or eight times as fast as the *pokok* melody, evenly filling in all sonic space. In order to play *kotekan* the musician must hear his part in relation to the complementary part, as one composite melody rather than in isolation. The player must damp the note just played, allowing his partner to strike his note in the space, so that the two are not sounding at the same time. It takes years to develop the required clean, rapid damping technique.

There are several types of *kotekan*, from simple onbeat/offbeat alternation to syncopated, complex patterning with seemingly endless permutations. Each type is linked with specific genres, gong structures, melodies, ensembles, and theatrical moods. Some are closely tied to the *pokok*, reinforcing, surrounding, or anticipating its pitches, while others float as a static pitch palette independent of the *pokok* melody. In *kebyar* compositions these types are often combined.

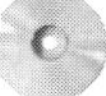

In CD tracks 18–20 you will hear the same portion of "Jaya semara" that you heard in the low instrument excerpt (activities 3.1 and 3.2). In each example, you will hear first the *polos* alone, then the *sangsih* alone, and then the two played together. The time-keeping gong keeps the beat, and the *ugal* plays the fundamental melody as a reference.

Single-Note Kotekan. In the most basic type of *kotekan* (called *norot*, meaning "to follow"), the figuration follows the movement of the *pokok* melody: both parts strike the *pokok* pitch together as an upbeat that anticipates the *pokok* pitch before it is played. The *polos* part subdivides the *pokok* pulse, repeating the *pokok* pitch, playing evenly on the beat. The *sangsih* part starts with the *polos* then immediately moves to the upper neighbor pitch (i.e., the metallophone key adjacent to the one the *polos* is playing), playing a continuous offbeat. The resulting figuration is a pivoting between *pokok* pitch and its upper neighbor. Some of my teachers have said that this type of *kotekan* connotes calmness. At slower tempos each player performs the composite of this figuration (i.e., both *pokok* and its upper neighbor pitch).

ACTIVITY 3.3 Kotekan norot

On CD track 18 you hear first the polos *part; at 0:32 the* sangsih *part; at 1:00 the composite.*

Begin by clapping the pokok *pulse. This is the same as the* kempli *timekeeper.*

Now try to clap the rhythm of the polos *part played on the* gangsas. *You will notice it strikes twice quickly before the strong beat, then it strikes three evenly spaced repeating notes before moving to another scale tone.*

When the sangsih *enters, try to clap its offbeat part.*

When both parts are played together, use both hands in alternation on a table or lap to "play" the composite.

Try to divide up the parts with classmates: one player plays the pokok *pulse, one claps the* polos, *and another the* sangsih *rhythms. Try to aim for an evenly spaced composite. The kotekan is notated in figure 3.1. I have tried to show the end-stress in my nonconventional use of western staff notation.*

In another simple type of *kotekan* the composite melody is divided by simple alternation between *polos* and *sangsih*. This type of *kotekan* is called *nyog-cag,* which means "leaping." The figuration leaps over and surrounds the *pokok* pitches, and *polos* and *sangsih* parts leap over each other. It is said to have a cheerful character.

ACTIVITY 3.4 Kotekan nyog-cag

On CD track 19 you hear first the polos *part; at 00:34 the* sangsih *part; at 1:04 the composite. As in activity 3.3, first try to clap the* pokok *or the* kempli *pulse. Then try to clap the*

FIGURE 3.1 *Transcription of* norot kotekan *("Jaya Semara"* pangecet*)*

polos *pulse (which doubles the* kempli *pulse). Then try to clap along with the* sangsih *part. You will notice that this is much harder than the* polos *part. In fact, this is rarely done in Bali because musicians hear the* sangsih *part as fitting into the composite rather than going against the main pulse as it does when played alone. When both parts play together notice that the composite is an even alternation of* polos *and* sangsih.

In the actual performance of this part of "Jaya Semara" the *gangsas* alternate between the two types of *kotekan*. You can hear an excerpt of this on CD track 20, the *pangecet* section of "Jaya Semara": the neighbor-tone, "following" *kotekan (norot)*, from 00:00, is followed by a brief break at 00:22; from 00:23 to the end of the excerpt there is "jumping" *kotekan* (*nyog-cag*).

Syncopated Patterning Kotekan. In other *kotekan* types each part consists of a pattern rather than a single note. These patterning types include *kotekan telu* (3) and *empat* (4), denoting the number of keys spanned by the figuration of both parts.

In *kotekan telu* (3) the *polos* and *sangsih* share a pitch around which each pivots, playing patterns which, when combined, result in a single-line melody (figure 3.2).

ACTIVITY 3.5 Kotekan telu *(3) from the piece "Jauk Manis"*

Listen to CD track 21. Pair up with a classmate and try to sing the repeating sixteen-beat melody played on the ugal *for the duration of the example. You will hear the* polos *part followed by the* sangsih *at 00:42; the composite at 1:11. Try clapping the rhythm of each part of the* kotekan. *Listen to CD track 22: the same* kotekan *is played up to tempo. Finally, on CD track 23 the same* kotekan *is played with the rest of the ensemble: it begins with a drum introduction; at 00:08 the* ugal *plays a melodic introduction; at 00:13 the* gangsas *enter and play the* kotekan.

FIGURE 3.2 *Transcription of* kotekan telu *"3" ("Jauk Manis")*

In *kotekan empat* (4) the melodic unit spans four keys, with *polos* usually consisting of the lower two and *sangsih* the upper two, and at certain points the outer two pitches are played simultaneously, resulting in syncopated accentuation. This is heard in activity 3.6.

Expansion and Contraction of a Kotekan *Pattern.* *Kotekan* is designed to accommodate the sudden fluctuation of tempo that frequently occurs in Balinese music. This is done through *expansion* and *contraction*: an elaborating melody may be played by all the *gangsas* together at a slow or medium tempo, the *sangsih* filling in at the *empat* ("4," i.e., an interval spanning four keys) at certain points of stress, and then the same melody is divided between two parts in *kotekan* as the tempo increases.

ACTIVITY 3.6 *Expansion and contraction with a* kotekan empat *(4) pattern*

To hear the expansion and contraction of a lyrical melody, follow along with the listening guide in an excerpt of the famous kebyar *dance piece "Teruna Jaya" (CD Track 24).*

00:00 ugal *introduction to phrase, rapid tempo*
00:02 gangsas *enter with* kotekan *(ends with break)*
00:17 *slow tempo,* polos *and* sangsih *parts play full versions of melody,* ugal *plays lyrical melody*
00:58 *tempo speeds up and parts divide to separate* polos *and* sangsih

Reyong ***Figuration: Melodic Interlocking and Percussive Accentuation.*** In the *reyong,* the gong-chime instrument played by four players seated in a row, two techniques embellish the melody while a third technique adds percussive accentuation. This last technique, known as *ocak-ocakan,* percussively follows the drums: the players strike the rim of the kettles with the wooden tips of the mallets and the boss with the parts of the mallets wrapped with string at points of emphasis. The contrasting sounds are described onomatopoetically as *kechek,* when the wooden tips are played on the rim, *byong,* an open stroke on the boss, *byot,* a short attack on the boss, and *jet,* a damped stroke on the boss. The open stroke *byong* results in a rich chord (figure 3.3).

FIGURE 3.3 *Transcription of* reyong *chord*

ACTIVITY 3.7 Reyong ocak-ocakan

CD tracks 25 and 26 are taken from the same excerpt of "Teruna Jaya" that you just heard for kotekan *contraction in rapid tempo. The* reyong, *drums, and cymbals work as a unit throughout the piece to reinforce dance movements in a percussive manner. In CD track 25 the* reyong *players play the syncopated* ocak-ocakan *part alone. In CD track 26 you hear the same segment with the full* gamelan, *as it would sound in performance. Notice the way the* reyong *and* ceng-ceng *articulate the drum patterns.*

Reyong interlocking figuration is similar to two of the *gangsa kotekan* types. One type closely follows the melody (and is also called *norot,* from "follow"), and the other uses interlocking syncopated patterns that span four kettles, similar to *kotekan empat* (4). The four players are essentially playing two pairs of interlocking parts: the first and second players' parts are doubled at the octave by the third and fourth players.

ACTIVITY 3.8 Reyong *syncopated interlocking patterns from "Topeng Keras" (chapters 4 and 5)*

In CD track 27 both parts are played separately then together. Try singing each part separately while "playing" the pattern on a table, in your mind seated at the instrument, with the kettles in ascending order from left (low) to right (high), alternating right and left hands. When the composite is played, try to focus on the outer notes of each pattern, which are played simultaneously (i.e., the lowest note of the lower part and the highest note of the upper part), and you will hear the syncopation brought to the foreground of the texture. It is played much slower here than it would be in performance. Imagine the players seated along the instrument. First the lower part is played alone by players 1 and 3 (beginning at 00:06; this pattern repeats at 00:17 and 00:29); players 2 and 4 play the upper part (beginning at 00:40; repeating at 1:03); then both parts are played together by all four musicians beginning at 1:15 with gongs and ugal *added.*

Norot reyong interlocking closely follows the *pokok,* dividing up the melody tones between the two pairs of players.

ACTIVITY 3.9 Reyong norot

CD track 28 is taken from the same section of "Jaya Semara" used in the other examples in this chapter, also played much slower than it would be in performance. See if you can hear the way the reyong *embellishes and closely follows the* pokok *in an evenly distributed rhythm and texture (i.e., it is not syncopated as in the previous example).*

00:00	kempli *(timekeeping gong)*
00:05	jublag *plays* pokok *(skeletal melody)*
00:19	reyong: *lower part alone four times (played by two* reyong *players: players 1 and 3)*
00:43	reyong: *upper part alone four times (played by two* reyong *players: players 2 and 4)*
1:08	reyong: *composite (four players)*
1:30	*tempo increased*

Comparison of Reyong *and* Trompong. If you compare the musical role in the ensemble, the overall sound, and the approach to making a melody in *trompong* and *reyong,* they will seem like totally unrelated instruments, yet they are constructed identically. In *reyong* the instrument is shared among four players whose cooperative interlocking works together to create a densely packed elaboration, while the *trompong* is one of the few solo melodic instruments in *gamelan,* and its elaboration melodies are smooth and linear. When you listen to CD tracks 25–28, try to visualize the four musicians seated tightly together along the *reyong,* each with only a few kettles at his or her disposal (figure 2.10). Then try to imagine the *trompong* placed in the front of the ensemble, the single player seated on his or her knees, widely reaching with two mallets to either end of the instrument, sometimes playing in octaves and sometimes alternating his hands to play melodic ornaments and a single melodic line, sometimes playfully twirling his mallets (figures 2.11 and 6.1, CD tracks 2–4 and 38).

LEADERSHIP, CUEING, AND ENSEMBLE INTERACTION

Clearly delineated musical roles within the ensemble form an interactive network (see Brinner 1995) primarily based on aural cues. By this I mean that all players must respond to cues given by a number of players, depending on what it is being cued. While the lead drummer holds the position of highest authority, there are other "leaders" within the ensemble that communicate with each other and with the rest of the ensemble. One of the two drummers controls the tempo and provides most of the aural cues while the *ugal* player (player of the largest *gangsa*) acts as intermediary and, following the drummer, gives visual cues, enabling the players to coordinate their articulation and dynamics precisely. The *trompong* player leads the *ugal* in pieces that have *trompong.* In some cases a dancer initiates cues. The lead drummer signals the group when they are about to begin a piece by giving a single *plak* stroke, upon which all players pick up their mallets in uniform motion, mallets poised over their instruments and ready to play.

Gaya *(Charismatic Gesture).* *Gaya* is a Balinese term for charisma and showing off. In music, it implies an extroverted display of virtuosity, confidence, and style. The musicians in a group strive for a uniform *gaya* in which their movements are so well coordinated that they seem to move as one musician with a single spirit. This is especially apparent in the *gangsa* and *reyong* sections, where their mallets seem to fly through the air as they articulate impossibly rapid interlocking figuration. At ends of phrases their arm movements are as one as they complete an accented tone, let their mallets move away from the key in an arc pattern, and bring their hands to rest near the keys until the start of another phrase. The communal spirit reaches near perfection in such musical moments.

The metallophone leader, one of a pair of *ugal* players, embellishes the *pokok* melody while cueing musicians (figures 2.5, 2.9, and 3.4 show only one *ugal* player). The closest thing there is to a visual conductor in *gamelan*, the *ugal* player flashes his *panggul* (mallet) in the air before striking a key, which he does with exaggerated elbow movements and a flick in the wrist to indicate dynamics, tempo, and sudden stopping and starting. People always remark on the *gaya* of each *ugal* player. The term *ugal* is usually used to designate musical role, instrument, and player.

When present in *gamelan gong kebyar,* the *trompong* player (gong-chime soloist) anticipates melodic changes and cueing, taking on part

FIGURE 3.4 Ugal *(left),* kempli *(center), and* gangsa *(right). Musicians from Gamelan Çudamani.*

of the role that is otherwise filled by the *ugal*. However, the *ugal* role is still essential in leading the metallophones in precise articulation.

CONCLUSION: PUTTING THE LAYERS TOGETHER

You are ready to hear the entire final section or *pangecet* (*c* is pronounced *ch*) of the piece "Jaya Semara." Even though the melody and figuration repeats throughout, the dynamic contrasts in this section give it its shape. With each repetition, changes imply forward motion. Throughout, *gangsas* and *reyong* play antiphonally, alternating playing loudly in each cycle while overall dynamics swell and wane. Thus they take turns being in the foreground of the musical texture. The final time through, everyone plays loudly together.

ACTIVITY 3.10 *Listening to the ensemble play together*

On CD track 16 the entrance of each instrument group is staggered to enable you to hear each of them one by one until finally the entire ensemble plays together. This is not done in performance. To review all of the instruments of the ensemble see chapter 2 and figure 2.5. By now you should have memorized their names. The entire piece is covered in chapter 6.

00:00	*Gongs (activity 2.4)*
00:21	*Low instruments (activity 3.1)*
1:10	Ugal *enters with embellishment of melody*
1:21	Gangsas *enter with "neighbor tone"* kotekan *(sequence as in activity 3.3), along with* reyong *(activity 3.9).*
1:42	*Break in* kotekan
1:46	*Switch to "leaping"* kotekan (gangsas *play loudly,* reyong *softer)*
2:07	*Break in* kotekan
2:11	*Repeat of sequence from 1:21* (reyong *plays loudly,* gangsas *softer, cut here)*

Now you should have a clear picture of *stratified polyphony*, the main ways of elaborating the *pokok*, and the instrument roles in *gong kebyar*.

The mutual dependency that the players have on their partner's part and on all of the reference points within the texture has illustrated the first theme of this book.

The second and third themes of the book, music's link to theater, dance, history, and ritual, are demonstrated in the next two chapters, as I explore the musical and cultural sources on which *kebyar* compositions draw. Balinese musicians and listeners know that the compositional process consists of musical borrowing, building on the work of others before them. They are familiar with the material that is being borrowed, and they know the references that are being made to theatrical and dance forms and to periods in Balinese history. They have an implicit understanding of the inter-*gamelan* and extramusical references when they hear new compositions. It is this kind of contextualization that gives music meaning and power.

CHAPTER 4

The World of Stories: Integration of Music, Dance, and Drama in Traditional Balinese Theater

Originally there was one gamelan—melad prana *(= cutting to the quick), the orchestra that accompanies* gambuh *performances . . . created by Smara, the god of love and his spouse Ratih, to be played by the divine beings in their heaven. On hearing this ensemble, each of the gods of the four quarters, followed by the gods and priests in the sky and then the demons in the underworld, created their own versions. A king of great power with words of magic had all seven copied and from him all the other kings of Middle earth obtained them.*

Aji gurnita (The Teachings of Music), in Vickers 1985: 146

The stories people create (myths, legends, folk tales, "history") are our exegesis for the world around us and frame our experience. In Bali, shadow puppet plays, masked dance dramas, and other forms of theater enact stories that explain how things such as superstitions and daily practices came to be. People retain vast numbers of stories in their minds, with great attention to detail. Stories are accessible and relevant to all strata of society. In all of my time in Bali, a day did not pass without hearing numerous stories from *bemo* (public transportation) drivers, music teachers, food sellers, friends, and specialists. The famous shadow master I Wayan Wija sees many aspects of shadow play stories as enactments of psychological states; the many battle scenes, for instance, symbolize inner struggle. Stories in Bali are allegories for real-life situations and are enacted at important moments in people's lives. They are completely integrated into the Balinese worldview; they are lived.

Each story is enacted in its own stylistic manner. Just as one associates the *Nutcracker* with ballet, for instance, one expects a Panji tale (see below) to be in the style of *gambuh,* or to be sung in a style of group chant (*kidung*). This is not to say that stories cannot be refashioned in newer media. The Indian *Mahabharata* and *Ramayana* stories are associated with the mythological period performed in shadow plays, but they are constantly performed in modern dance dramas. However, it is important first to understand the primary associations for these art forms before approaching an understanding of how the "standard" has been subverted in new creations.

In this chapter and the next I introduce you to some of the theatrical traditions and their musical elements. These are important in themselves, but their relevance also extends beyond the boundaries of theatrical performances. Balinese listeners automatically feel the sense of drama or mood in their reception of nontheatrical music as well. Although there are purely instrumental pieces, most music is never completely divorced from its historical and dramatic associations.

PLAYING THE PAST IN THE PRESENT

Balinese performers and scholars conceive of stories, theater, dance, vocal genres, and ensembles as fitting into the three broad historical periods outlined in chapter 1 (Old, Middle and New). Figure 4.1 "fills in" the chart presented in figure 1.5 with examples of *gamelan,* theater, and dance associated with each period covered here. *Gamelan* ensembles are closely linked to dramatic forms. *Gambuh,* for instance, is the name of both the dramatic form and the musical ensemble that accompanies it. Sometimes the prefix *pa-* and affix *-an* surround the term designating the dance form, for instance, *pagambuhan* for *gambuh* and *palegongan* for *legong.*

Myths and legends offer explanations of the origins of certain *gamelan,* linking gods and kings. Today *gamelan* remain symbols of refinement and courtly life. Two lineages emerge from legends. *Gamelan* from the Old category of Balinese music history, associated with priests meditating in the forest, are said to predate Hindu Javanese influence. *Gambuh* and its seven descendents from the Middle category in the quote above are associated with Hindu-Java and were performed in the Balinese courts.

Genres in the Old Category: Sacred Ensembles. Many of the Old genres are associated with priestly activities and *Bali Aga* communities. These are isolated and rare communities that still follow indigenous Balinese practices that predate Hindu-Javanese influence. The architec-

Tua (Old) Kediri period Associated with priests	*Madya* (Middle) Gelgel period Associated with courts	*Baru* (New) 20th century and contemporary Village and academy based
Considered to be the oldest; often associated with *Bali Aga* communities (no Javanese influence)	Thought to have developed out of the Hindu-Javanese-modeled courts of Majapahit established in Bali between the 9th and 16th centuries; associated with *Kawi* (Old Javanese) narratives (poetic texts)	Developed from ensembles of the Middle category in the 20th century to the present
Narratives: *Mahabharata* and *Ramayana;* Buddhist tales	Narratives: Panji, Erlangga, and other stories telling of early Hindu Javanese-Balinese links; historical chronicles	Narratives: All stories from the later periods; pieces and dances free of narrative associations
The most sacred *(wali),* closely linked to ritual activities	Ceremonial *(bebali),* revered and performed alongside but not in ritual	Usually performed in secular contexts *(balih-balihan)*
No drums, *rebab,* or *suling;* mostly slab-type instruments rather than gong-chime	Drums, *rebab,* and *suling* important; many ensembles thought to have developed from *gambuh* (melody played on large, bamboo flutes)	Drums even more prominent; ensembles tend to be larger, louder, and music virtuosic and in fast tempos
Examples: four sacred ensembles including *salunding, gambang,* and two others (see McPhee); also *gender wayang;* an old form of *angklung*	Examples: *gambuh, semar pagulingan, palegongan (legong) gong gede, balaganjur (bebonangan* or "marching" *gamelan), topeng* masked dance drama	Examples: *gong kebyar, arja* (sung dance drama), *janger* (social singing of boys and girls), contemporary *balaganjur,* a newer form of *angklung, baris* and free dances, *kecak*

FIGURE 4.1 *Balinese conception of the periods of* gamelan, *dance, and theater*

ture, village layout, and customs differ dramatically from those typical of most Balinese villages. Four types of rare, sacred seven-tone ensembles are mostly restricted to these communities. Legends tell of supernatural means by which the *gamelan* came to each village. Only initiated members of the community may play these *gamelan,* and only during specified ceremonies because of their sacred nature. Many of the melodies in these repertoires are played to summon specific deities. The four types of sacred ensembles share pieces that are derived from sacred vocal chant in the Kawi language, which in former times they accompanied. Nowadays the instrumental and vocal music are performed separately, though they remain linked in the minds of the performers. Certain techniques such as rhythmic and *kotekan* patterns that are trademarks of these ensembles are frequently drawn from these and inserted in twentieth-century and contemporary creations. These borrowed musical features immediately reference the ensembles.

Sometimes ensembles and practices do not fit neatly into one of the three historical categories in real life. *Gamelan gender wayang,* the quartet that accompanies the *wayang kulit* (shadow puppet theater, the only Old category ensemble covered here) is such an example (CD tracks 5 and 29). Specialists consider it Old because of its sacred associations and some documentation; its primary association, however, is with the Hindu epics that it accompanies (*Mahabharata* and *Ramayana*), also placing it in the Middle category. Furthermore, performance context is just as important as ensemble type: *gender wayang* is played in the inner courtyard and considered *wali* for daytime ceremonial *wayang* (Preface photo); it is played in the middle courtyard for some night performances, and it can be played on the side of the road for other night performances that serve more of an entertainment function. Certain sacred dances and rites, such as a women's offering dance for the gods and women's sacred interlocking bamboo rice pounding done at ceremonies, are also considered Old (*Bali Aga)* and have carried over into widespread Hindu Balinese practices. Along with *gender wayang* they stand as living examples of pre-Hindu indigenous and Hindu-Bali syncretism.

Genres in the Middle Category: The Hindu Javanese Legacy. In the Middle category are ensembles and dance/theater forms associated with the early Hindu Balinese courts that had links with Hindu Java. Though associated with Java and with certain broadly shared features of Javanese instruments and forms, no one knows whether they are really preservations of what Javanese performance was like in those days, since the two cultures have subsequently diverged drastically. Music and dance vocabulary from this Middle category are the basis for most contemporary music and dance forms. Two distinct types of ensembles within this category have spawned other ensembles. The first is *gamelan gambuh* (mentioned in the quote beginning this chapter) and the dance drama it accompanies (CD track 8); the other is *gamelan gong gede* (the "great gong" ensemble), known primarily for its long, stately *gending lalambatan* (slow instrumental compositions) played at temple ceremonies.

The *gambuh* ensemble accompanies the *gambuh* dance drama enacting the Panji cycle of tales emanating from medieval east Java (see below). In *gambuh* the melody is played on four large bamboo *suling* (vertical flutes) and *rebab* (spike fiddle). It sounds strikingly different from other *gamelan* because there are no metallophones or gong-chimes. Elements such as gong structures, drum patterns, and the flute melody (*pokok*) of *gambuh* were transferred to the bronze ensembles, transforming their sound.

The ensembles belonging to each of the "gods of the four quarters" noted in the *Aji Gurnita,* the treatise quoted above, were originally named after various actions of Semara, the god of love. For instance, the bronze ensemble that many *gambuh* compositions were directly transferred to is *gamelan semar pagulingan* (CD track 38). The name of this delicate instrumental ensemble played in the king's bedchamber translates as "the god of love sleeping." *Semar patangian,* "the god of love rising," was the original name for the *gamelan* accompanying the *legong* dance form, now known as *gamelan palegongan.* These and others represent the embodiment of the god's activities in *gamelan.* The idea of putting ritual into motion as sound and movement is central in Bali. *Gamelan semar pagulingan,* the ensemble you will hear in chapter 6, has a seven-tone *pelog* tuning (*saih-pitu,* "series of seven"). Similar to *gong kebyar* in its stratified polyphonic layered texture, its instruments are smaller and more delicate than the large, loud instruments of *kebyar.* Its melodic leader is the *trompong* (gong-chime row). The two-stringed spike fiddle, *rebab,* is easily heard through the delicate texture, evoking refinement.

Legong is danced by three prepubescent girls and often involves trance (discussed below). The ensemble (*gamelan palegongan*) is similar to *semar pagulingan,* but two to four *gender rambat* (twelve- to thirteen-keyed delicate metallophones played with two mallets) replace the *trompong* as melodic leaders, and the seven-tone tuning of *semar pagulingan* is reduced to a pentatonic tuning in *palegongan.*

Like the *gambuh* dance drama, *legong* stories evoke medieval Javanese legends of early contacts between Javanese and Balinese nobility. The character and dance vocabulary of the maidservant (the *condong*) to the princess or queen in *gambuh* has been transmitted to one of the three main characters in *legong.* Most female dance styles base their movement vocabulary on those of *gambuh* and *legong.*

Gamelan gong gede ensembles are rare today. They consist of huge, heavy bronze instruments, many sets of metallophones, and several sets of gong-chime instruments. A *gong gede* ensemble can number some forty-five musicians, with weighty timbre and compositional style. Many compositional devices of modern *gamelan gong kebyar* (*gamelan gong*) are derived from those of this older ensemble. Its characteristic features are drums played with a mallet in the player's right hand, giving a booming timbre to the drumming, a group of large, handheld crash cymbals (*ceng-ceng kopyak*), and long, stately, slow compositions played at temple ceremonies.

Gamelan gong accompanies *topeng*, a male form of masked dance drama. *Topeng* plays enact historical chronicles, a later period in Balinese history from that of *legong*, but also belonging to the Middle category (see below). Most male dance movements are derived from this form.

Genres in the New Category: Drawing from Middle and Old and Breaking Free. Ensembles and genres of the third, New category for the most part have developed from those of the Middle category, but new ensembles and dance styles that are free of Middle-period associations are constantly being created, and it has become popular to draw from the Old category for new compositions. One major distinction between this period and the Middle-period is that music and dance may be free from any narrative associations. Rather than tell a story, they may portray a mood or character or activity such as the changing moods of a youth, amorous bumblebees, or dances once popular in the 1950s and 1960s that promoted themes such as weaving or harvesting. Not all new music and dance is non-narrative, however. On the contrary, the *Mahabharata* and *Ramayana* remain mainstays of performance even today when performed with entirely new formats.

***The Idea of Completeness: Revisiting* Ramé.** As you learned in chapter 1, theatrical traditions are closely linked to ceremonies in Balinese life. An important ideal exists that in order for a ceremony to be complete, genres from several periods must be performed. Temple committees discuss and decide what performing arts genre should be performed in any given ceremony, and their members do not always agree. The choice of any given genre is often locally situated (i.e., it varies from place to place). One guideline that some specialists use is that actually five periods of history ought to be represented at any "complete" ceremony, rather than the three broad ones outlined above. Theoretically, each historical period would be represented by several criteria such as the story, the language, or the musical accompaniment. But it is also generally understood that it is rare to have a truly "complete" ceremony, and as long as the periods are symbolically represented in some way, people just make do with what is available to them. Remember that the sense of *ramé* is of utmost importance: sonic spaces are filled with sound, physical space with people and movement, the air with incense, and the present with references to Bali's past.

One way this sense of completeness is achieved is to have sacred vocal genres that represent distinct time periods. For example, *kekawin* is a type of sung poetry in the Kawi (Old Javanese) language that has come to represent the Middle category of Hindu-Javanese influence (chapter 1). Other historical periods including Indian, early, and recent Balinese are represented in chant forms (such as *kidung*, associated with Prince Panji, mentioned above). When all else fails, some communities (in village temples and private house ceremonies) resort to boom boxes that play (often distorted) recordings of the desired *gamelan* or vocal genre. On one occasion, one of my teachers played a recording of an Old category ensemble that never would have been played in his village. He was well aware of this but told me that it just felt right to add it to the blend of live ensembles because of its "old Bali" sacred associations.

Figure 4.2 illustrates how some genres fit into the schema of five periods of history represented in the Balinese present. In some ways the divisions are arbitrary because art forms develop far more gradually than these abrupt, ossified periods. (Similar problems have been found

Association	CD track	Performing art genre, story, and language
Indian	2	Sloka chant of priest, Sanskrit language
Hindu Javanese and Indian	5	*Wayang* (done as a daytime ceremonial *wayang lemah*), *Mahabharata*, mixture of Sanskrit, Kawi, and modern Balinese languages
Hindu Javanese	8	*Gambuh* dance drama, Kawi language, or *legong*, Kawi narration both with Panji tales
Balinese History	6 & 7	*Topeng* (masked dance drama), historical chronicles, Balinese language
Modern Bali	10, 11, 39, & 40	*Gong kebyar*, dance drama *(sendratari)*, drama gong, could have Balinese-language narration

FIGURE 4.2 *Historical associations of the performing arts*

by musicologists with the Western categories of Baroque, Classical, Romantic, and so forth.) The important point to note here is that performance in Bali has historical relevance, even if the actual dates and time periods overlap. The reenactment of a time and the simultaneity of performance are what are important: the playing of the past in the present.

ASSUMPTIONS AND CONVENTIONS IN TRADITIONAL BALINESE THEATER

Every form of theater has its conventions. The spectator must be familiar with these in order to know how to behave and how to fully appreciate a performance. The conventions are based on larger cultural assumptions that are expressed in numerous media, theater being only one of them. In this section you are introduced to underlying cultural assumptions and theatrical conventions having to do with the concept of a "story," accessibility of a given genre, and the role of the interpreter in what I am calling "traditional Balinese theater," meaning performance practices that predate Western influences of the twentieth century, for the most part.

The Concept of a "Story": Orality and Literacy in Performance. It is fundamental to traditional Balinese theater that only a kernel of a story is told in a single performance. While the overall plot schema of an entire epic can be summarized in a telling, theatrical genres take only fragments of the story line and embellish them, rather than playing out an entire story to its conclusion. There are endless permutations, versions, and variants of tales. Shadow puppet masters and other storytellers throughout Southeast Asia use a tree metaphor to describe this process. The main, precomposed aspect of the story is the trunk, while in performance individuals are free to compose and enact their own branch and twig tales that relate to those of the trunk. The "trunks," preserved in texts such as a ninth-century Sanskrit version of the *Ramayana* or Old Javanese Kawi poems, are retained as poetry from which performers may quote during performance. The entire poem is never sung, however. One reason is that, while performers possess palm-leaf manuscripts containing the literary works, their primary relationship with the texts is oral, and people do not memorize the entire text from beginning to end. This oral approach to written texts is shared throughout Southeast Asia. Unlike traditions that rely exclusively on oral transmission, however, parts of the poems are embedded as references to enrich the performance, to establish the performer's legitimacy, and to connect the present performance to all past tellings of the story.

In any given performance the plot is usually not the main focus. Rather, the elaborations, digressions, and manner of execution take precedence. The number of complex, convoluted plot twists, interrelated stories, characters, and genealogies that performers retain in their minds is positively astounding. People generally have their own versions of stories with which they are intimately familiar, yet they are also aware of the story's numerous permutations as performed by others. There is no single, correct "way the story goes" because its path is not predictable. It is the variations that intrigue the audience and performers.

The Panji Cycle. The Panji cycle, depicted in *gambuh* and *legong*, serves as an example. The cycle includes numerous versions and variants of stories of mistaken identity, magic, and romance. The basic characters include Prince Panji, who is in love with the princess of Daha. One version has it that an evil imposter takes on the form of the princess and is about to wed Prince Panji when the actual princess disguises herself as a man, enters the palace, and stops the wedding in time. The princess is abducted in numerous ways, depending on the version. In one she wanders off chasing butterflies, gets lost, and is then taken in by a king who pursues her romantically; in another she vanishes suddenly on her and Prince Panji's wedding night. At the start of the story Panji has a different name, and only after he has set out on his journey to find her does he take on a new identity and rename himself Panji. Most stories are branches of this main one, following Panji on his long and magical journey. Panji is a folk hero whose attributes and faults are well known, and references to him are made regularly in ritual and daily life. One version has it that the Lasem story performed in *legong* is one episode of the larger Panji tale (see *legong* below). Stories are allegories for human situations. For instance, the story "Panji's Haircutting" is sung during the ceremonial haircutting portion of wedding ceremonies and is laden with symbolism.

Levels of Abstraction and Accessibility. The way a story is played out and its accessibility depend on the performance medium. In *gambuh* there is a distance between performers and audience. The stories evoke a distant past, and the dance form is abstract. A number of highly stylized character dances precede the drama, which unfolds gradually.

The language used is Old Javanese (Kawi), and there is no interpreter to translate the narrative into Balinese. For most audience members it is considered esoteric, its popularity restricted to literati, yet in theory it is still valued by most people.

Legong's portrayal of the story is also abstract, but in a different way. Its main focus is the dance, choreographed perhaps in the nineteenth century but updated in the twentieth century when versions of it became more or less fixed in each locale. The spectator's interest is in the way the dancer moves and the relationship between *gamelan* and dance. There are no points during the performance where the dance stops to portray drama as there is in *gambuh*. *Legong* is immensely popular, and it is the main dance that young girls learn to obtain the basic female dance movements.

Topeng masked dance drama enacts semilegendary historical chronicles (*babad*) of Hindu-Balinese kings, their ministers, and high priests. Although some stories take place during the same era as those of *gambuh*, the performance style of *topeng* is totally distinct. *Topeng* is an extremely direct, down-to-earth medium and hence very popular.

The Role of Interpreters. The role of intermediaries is essential to many forms of Balinese theater. The *topeng* stories are "told" through intermediaries—bawdy comic servants wearing half-masks who act as translators for silent noble characters wearing full masks. While the numerous plots usually involve a king who is confronted by some problem such as a foreign invasion and his resolution of the problem, the main focus is on the comic scenes that occur between action scenes. These can be quite extensive conversations between two comic characters who argue with each other, discuss local gossip and current events, and subvert standard protocol by mocking the nobility. The intermediaries recontextualize and bring the story up to date. Often the humor is in the disjunction between the two eras: the noble reverence for kings and ministers and the extremely banal humor of the modern buffoons.

The role of narrator held by the *dalang* (a trained shadow master) is central in the *wayang kulit* (shadow puppet theater). Some non-*wayang* traditional theater genres have a trained *dalang* acting as narrator. He is known as the *juru tandak* (master narrator) in this case, yet he draws on some of the literary and vocal references from his *wayang* training. *Legong*, for instance, usually has a *juru tandak* who sits in the midst of the *gamelan* and sings oblique poetic narration. He is not visible or prominent but simply adds to the musical texture and timbre.

A more recent form of dance drama, *sendratari* (see chapter 7), which first appeared in Java in 1961, has departed from the traditional theatrical standards by enacting complete epics in summary, with a prominent *juru tandak* providing narration and dialogue for all the characters. This form is extremely accessible and popular in Bali, drawing crowds of thousands to witness the *Mahabharata* and *Ramayana*. Its popularity shows the audience's willingness to accept certain nontraditional aesthetic values in this condensed form of storytelling. My *wayang* teachers attribute this to the influence of fast-paced Western media such as TV and film. In fact, this theatrical form was created for tourist consumption and only later became incorporated into regular Balinese practice. But performers and audiences recognize its distinction from "traditional" Balinese forms. Even in these altered forms of storytelling there remains enough material from traditional performance, such as the timbre and language of the narrator's voice, evoking *wayang* and other genres, to be acceptable and familiar.

Genres of Theater. Of the numerous forms of traditional Balinese theater, the most frequently performed are listed in figure 4.3. The chart shows the associated story and where it takes place or originates, the musical ensemble, and its tuning system. It also identifies those with a *dalang*, those with an interpreter, and the primary actors. Although this volume only introduces *wayang kulit* (shadow puppet theater), *legong*, *topeng*, and briefly, *calonarang*, it is important that you are aware of the others. Figure 4.3 is roughly organized according to musical ensemble and chronological order.

There is some overlap of ensemble, repertoire, and story among several of these forms; they are interrelated. For instance, the *barong* is one of the most important characters in dance drama in Bali. Danced by two dancers (one wearing the masked head and front legs, the other in the rear legs), this dragonlike creature is the protector of the village. Every village or neighborhood has its own *barong* that is housed in a temple, as it is a sacred object even when not being danced. Notice on the chart that *barong*, *calonarang*, and *jauk* share some features in accompaniment and story. The *barong* has its own set of stories as well as being an intrinsic part of the *calonarang* dance drama enacting the battle between the evil witch Rangda and the *barong*, often done in graveyards for exorcistic purposes and involving trance. The ensemble that accompanies these dances is usually the same one that accompanies *legong*—*gamelan palegongan*. In the next section I will introduce you to *wayang kulit*, and in chapter 5 I will focus on the other two genres, *topeng* and *legong*.

Genre	Story	Ensemble	Tuning	D/I	Actors
Wayang kulit	*Mahabharata* or *Ramayana*	*Gender wayang* quartet; *gamelan batel*	S	D	Shadow puppets
Gambuh	Panji (Java)	*Gamelan gambuh:* several large *suling, rebab, kendang,* colotomic gongs, other percussion	P7	D	Men, now women too; speak
Legong	Variety: *Ramayana,* historical Javanese	*Gamelan palegongan*	P	(D)	3 young girls; silent
Barong	Balinese, protector of village, danced by two dancers similar to Chinese dragon	*Gamelan palegongan* or *gamelan gong*	P	—	men, mask; silent, trance
Calonarang	Erlangga, east Java 11th cent., Rangda the witch fights Barong	*Gamelan palegongan*	P	(D/I)	men, now women too; silent, trance
Jauk	*Mahabharata; barong* story	*Gamelan gong*	P	(I)	men; masks
Arja	Romances; Panji stories	*Gamelan arja:* singing, 1 or 2 small *suling,* 2 small drums, small *ceng-ceng,* 2 struck bamboo zithers	P/S	I	men and women; stylized speech & song—Balinese language in Javanese meters
Baris	military, many types, *(Ramayana)*	*Gamelan gong*	P	(D)	1–60 boys/men; no speech or song
Topeng	Balinese historical chronicles	*Gamelan gong*	P	(D/I)	men, now women too; masks, stylized speech/song

Key:
Tuning: P = five-tong pelog; *P7 = seven-tone* pelog; S = slendro
D/I:D = dalang *(also called* juru tandak*); I = interpreter; ( ) = optional*

FIGURE 4.3 *The most frequently performed genres of Balinese theater*

WAYANG KULIT (SHADOW PUPPET THEATER)

ACTIVITY 4.1 *As you read this section on* wayang kulit, *consider the ways in which Balinese audiences experience theater and the important role of* wayang *in Balinese culture.*

Sukawati Village, 1990: My teacher, Pak Loceng, is a master of *gender wayang*, the instrument that is played in a quartet to accompany shadow puppet theater (figure 1.6). *Gender wayang* also accompanies certain rites of passage such as toothfiling and cremation ceremonies (see Gold 1990, 1998). Performers say this is because of its *wayang* associations. Known as *wayang kulit* (shadow puppets made of rawhide), the puppets are intricately carved and silhouetted against a screen lit by the flame of a flickering coconut oil lamp (figures 4.4, 4.5, and 4.6, and Preface Photo). *Wayang* is a necessary component of most religious ceremonies and also an extremely popular form of dramatic entertainment.

FIGURE 4.4 *The shadow side of a* wayang kulit *performance. Twalen & Merdah (left), Kayon (center), and Delem & Sangut (right).* (Photo by Lisa Gold.)

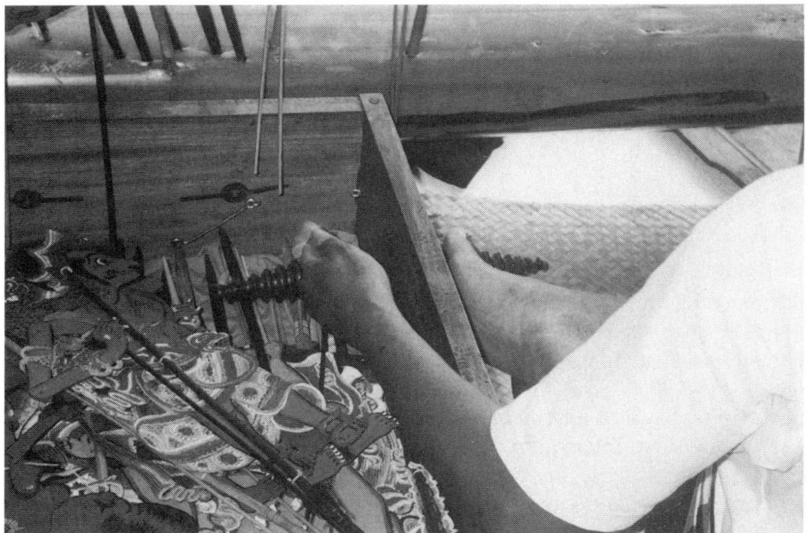

FIGURE 4.5 Dalang *Ida Bagus Buduk striking puppet box with* cepala *(wooden beater), one held in hand, another between his toes.* (*Photo by Lisa Gold.*)

On the day of the *wayang* the *gender wayang* players accompanied a toothfiling ceremony, one of the most significant rites of passage that all Balinese undergo. It was held in the family compound for young adult children of the host family. A special ritual tooth filer symbolically filed the six upper teeth, including the canines, that symbolically contain the "six enemies of mankind" or the "six vices." The playing of the *gender wayang*, chanting of *kidung*, and ceremonial actions help the ritual participant to control these vices. Its other purpose is to distinguish humans from demons, who have fangs, so that when humans die they will be accepted in the heavenly realm. This ceremony must be done prior to death, but is often combined with a wedding ceremony of one of the siblings.

The host family sponsored an evening *wayang* as a form of entertainment for family, guests, and villagers, to be held in the village community center near the house. My teacher would accompany a very famous *dalang* (shadow master/spiritual practitioner) who always draws a huge crowd because of his ability to combine ancient philosophy with modern themes while telling jokes and manipulating the puppets in

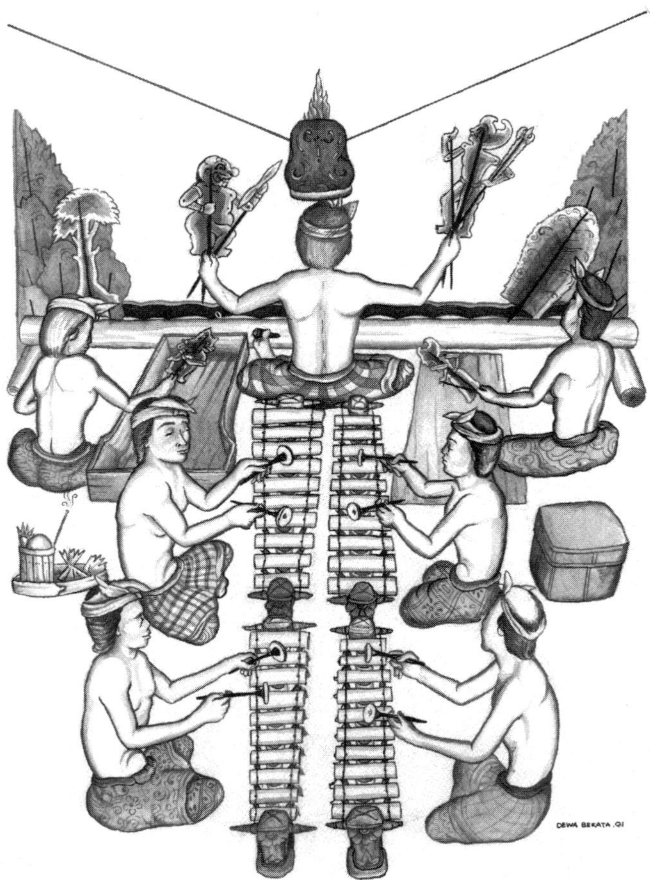

FIGURE 4.6 Wayang *setting: The* dalang *(shadow master) sits before the center of the large, white cotton* wayang *screen, which is illuminated by a coconut-oil lamp hanging at the center of the screen above his head. He is flanked on either side by two assistants. Behind him sits the quartet of* gender wayang *players, who provide crucial musical support throughout the performance.* *(Drawing by I Dewa Putu Berata.)*

artfully choreographed battle scenes. Although the audience may eat, drink, gamble, and gossip during a performance, when this *dalang* performs his audience sits riveted. He brings audiences to tears and uproarious laughter.

The **Dalang.** *Dalang* say that keeping a large audience interested and entertained while preserving the character of the stories is a challenge in today's fast-paced world. But keeping the audience there until the end means that the *wayang* was successful and, in turn, that the ceremony will also be a success; there is much at stake. *Dalang* have multiple roles: they entertain, they are the repository of knowledge for the community, and through rigorous spiritual training they are masters of powerful *mantras* and magical powers. Some *dalang,* specially trained as priest-*dalang,* conduct ceremonies following the performance, as well as ceremonial *wayang* that serve exorcistic, healing, or other purposes. Hired by a village or by private families, they are invited to perform *wayang* for purposes that extend beyond entertainment. Intertwined with a performance's success as a purely aesthetic experience is its success in its ritual efficacy. When a *dalang* is able to keep the audience interested until the story ends, this important connection between the *wayang* world and the human realm is made. If a family cannot afford to hire an entire *wayang* troupe they will go to the home of the *dalang,* who performs the necessary rites while holding certain puppets.

In *wayang* performance the *dalang* has a central role and is a storyteller par excellence. His voice speaks and sings for all characters and narration. He controls the entire performance by cueing the musicians to play certain mood and character pieces that may stop or start instantaneously. He artfully manipulates dozens of characters. Memorized poetic texts are combined with improvised speech as the *dalang* weaves together a complex story of plots, subplots, and digressions with comedy, action, dance, and music framing the tale. The basic stories, drawn from the *Mahabharata* and the *Ramayana* for the most part, are well known to the audience, yet each performance is unique and cannot be replicated. The *dalang* never performs a story exactly the same way twice, and he is free to compose "branch" and "twig" tales that diverge from the original Sanskrit epic "trunk."

The *dalang* uses many languages and language levels in *wayang* performance. The noble characters speak only the esoteric Kawi known by few audience members; additionally there are several "levels" of the Balinese language that indicate the hierarchical caste system. Commoners must speak high Balinese to members of a higher caste. Nobles speak in low Balinese to commoners. Conversations between same-caste characters are in a shared language level.

The *dalang* controls the performance by giving cues to the musicians. There are a number of ways he does this: sitting cross-legged, he holds a wooden beater in his right foot between his toes (figure 4.5). With this he strikes the box that holds the puppets, placed to his left. He holds in his left hand another mallet, which he uses when that hand is not holding a puppet. He can also give verbal and sung cues, and the musicians anticipate the desired piece from the dramatic context.

The *dalang* has a general sense of the progression of a story before performing, and he has in his mind a set of *gender wayang* pieces and sung poetry available to him that provide dramatic support as a framework for plot construction. But he is free to put together scenes and dialogue spontaneously. This sort of spontaneous performance is widespread in Southeast Asian oral narrative genres. The storyteller or actor is able to "improvise" long, complex stories by drawing from a storehouse of memorized chunks of material (formulas) and assembling them differently each time. This form of oral narrative, known in Western scholarship as *oral formulaity*, applies to all forms of traditional Balinese theater. The *dalang* has a heavier load than most actors however, because he must carry the entire performance alone, along with his supportive *gender* players. Furthermore, the well-being of the household, village, or town that sponsors the *wayang* is in the hands of the *dalang*. Therefore, the choice of story and its execution must be fitting with the situation.

Categories of *gender wayang* pieces provide the needed dramatic support. There are short, rapid pieces that accompany puppet movement; even faster, syncopated pieces for battle; slow, rhythmically free pieces for mood songs such as sadness, romance, and contemplation; and numerous character pieces.

Four of the most important characters, indigenous to Bali and not from the Indian epics, are the comic servants who function as interpreters. They translate the esoteric Kawi language of the nobility into local Balinese. Two pairs of servants, one translating for the "good" characters, or protagonists (on the *dalang's* right), and the other for the "evil" characters, or those opposing the actions of the former (on his left), interject humorous dialogue scenes. On the right are the revered old servant Twalen and his son Merdah; on the left are the egotistical Delem and his quick-witted younger brother, Sangut. These highly revered comic servants represent the mouthpiece of the *dalang* and the voice of the community. They discuss current politics, local gossip, and other topics considered inappropriate in everyday discourse. In this sense the *dalang* speaks through them, using the tale as a framework for the larger issues at hand.

The Progression of a Performance. In Balinese performance there is a gradual progression from the everyday world into the world of the performance. This progression represents a multiphased, transformative experience for the performers and audience. In a sense, "the performance" for a Balinese *dalang* has already begun the moment he leaves his home. At this important juncture he is already silently intoning inner *mantras* while going through a number of other internal preparations that focus his thoughts on the performance and bring him in touch with the forces of the *wayang* world he is about to enter.

As we arrived at the home of the host who sponsored the *wayang*, it was immediately apparent that the roles that the members of the *wayang* troupe have during performance exist socially, outside of the performance context as well. While sitting in the host's home the *dalang* is surrounded by his assistants and musicians, clearly taking center stage in the polite conversation with the host. I was amazed to watch him tell stories and exhibit his knowledge with verbal adroitness. Periodically he would break into song, quoting a Kawi poem from a didactic treatise to illustrate a philosophical point. While doing this, the *dalang* was also gaining important information about the situation of the performance context that he would later incorporate into his telling of the story. The assistants were making the cotton wick to be used in the oil lamp during the *wayang*. The musicians would chime in (so to speak) now and then, deferring to the *dalang*. The ebb and flow of this portion of the evening seemed to mirror or foretell the performance yet to come as the mood would seamlessly shift from somber to reflective to jovial. A sense of expansive time was created in this generous hosting period prior to performance. The highly formalized protocol of social interaction also exists within the performance structure.

After the meal the musicians and assistants went to the performance platform outside of the house to finish stretching the screen on a frame and hanging the oil lamp. The musicians began playing. My teacher's *gender wayang* group is known as one of the best in Bali, so crowds began to gather to listen to their "sitting pieces," instrumental compositions played before the shadow master takes his seat.  (In CD track 29 you hear an excerpt of "Sekar Sungsang," a sitting piece named after a type of flower played by renowned *gender* musicians of another village, Tunjuk, Tabanan.) I settled down behind my teacher so I could watch the play from the musicians' and *dalang's* side while most of the audience watched the shadows on the white screen, where "special effects" such as magical transformations are really believable. During the piece the *dalang* lit the coconut-oil lamp hanging in front of his face and set it swinging so that the shadows could come to life and appear to be breathing. All components of the stage set-up are symbolic: the screen is said to divide the seen (*sekala*) from the unseen (*niskala*). It also represents the world and the heavens; the lamp is the sun and the banana log at the base of the screen in which puppets are planted is the earth. The *dalang*, representing God and sitting in the center, works a kind of magic on the crowd as he spins his tales accompanied by the sound of the *gender wayang*.

When he is ready to "begin" he raps on the puppet box three times, with a *mantra* invites the puppets to dance, and signals the musicians to switch to the beginning of the *wayang* overture. This is a long, multisectional piece played while the *dalang* takes the puppets out of the box one by one and lines them up along the banana log while deciding what story he will perform that night. The final piece in the suite is called "Eel's Bones" after the curvy melody played in the left-hand (CD track 5 to 00:38). Two dances of a sacred tree of life puppet known as the *kayon* are followed by numerous opening invocations calling forth the voices to enter the puppets. You can hear the beginning of the second *kayon* dance at 00:38 to 1:18. At 00:51 you will hear the *dalang* striking the puppet box with his wooden beater to cue the musicians to accompany the *kayon* puppet's movements. The *gender wayang* part features a left-hand ostinato, quick tempo, and the right-hand alternation of simple pivoting between two pitches and delicate *kotekan*. This form is *batel*, related to a similar form played on large ensembles (chapter 5). It provides excitement and agitation fitting for battle scenes and the spirited energy of this puppet.

His opening song, "Alas harum" ("The Fragrant Forest," CD track 5 at 1:18), evokes the five Pandawa brothers as they march into the final battle. Its text is drawn from the last book of the *Mahabharata* and recalls a tragic scene. All *wayang* that perform *Mahabharata* stories begin with this song, regardless of where in the epic the particular story takes place. Thus it casts a somber shadow over the play that is about to begin and links the present story to all others before it. It is well into the second hour of the performance that the story "begins," yet, the performance really began long before that.

Both audience and performers have spent at least an hour, in a sense, preparing for this moment. This preparation points to a fundamental distinction between traditional Balinese and Western theater conventions. In the West, most performances have a specified time of beginning, clearly marked by numerous conventions such as a curtain opening, and the audience's focused attention to the actors on the stage. The audience is a clearly delineated group that is distinguished from the performers. These boundaries and roles, which are cultural assumptions for Western theatergoers, are irrelevant in Bali because of a basic integration of the arts into life that operates on multiple levels simultaneously. Rather than a unilateral, linear experience for the audience, there are shifting focal points such as music, movement, humor, and visiting with friends, eating, or drinking.

Taksu: ***Divine Inspiration and "Shifting Focal Points."*** If the *dalang* has *taksu* that night, then the audience will be moved to tears and laughter and the performance will be successful. *Taksu* is the divine inspiration that overcomes performers during the act of performance. They do not always attain this inner state, but it is the desired one. People say that when *taksu* takes over they are unaware of what they say or do, but it is a different experience from going into trance. Audience members can sense when a performer has *taksu*. Performers say that *taksu* does not depend on how good a performer is. Some less competent *dalang* can have it one night for no apparent reason. It is noted to occur for dancers and *dalang*, probably because it is a personal experience that happens to the individual. Ensemble musicians generally do not speak of having *taksu*, but rather of the importance of group unity and precision.

Performers balance three elements, the *trikaya parisuda*, or "Three Good Acts": *bayu*, "energy, physical action"; *sabda*, "speech, or voice, of important persons, of a supreme being"; and *idep*, "thought, mind" (Dibia 1992, glossary). These are three equal qualities that must be combined when doing anything. I Wayan Dibia discusses them as the "three powers" that form the basis of changing "aesthetic focal points" in Balinese performance. In *wayang*, for instance, *bayu* is movement, *sabda* is verbal and vocal artistry, and *idep* is the conceptualization of the story (Zurbuchen 1987: 129). The way the audience is expected to respond is an inseparable component of shifting focal points; they are expected, for instance, to be aware of several activities occurring simultaneously, to "tune in and out" throughout the performance. The audience is also expected to respond verbally or with laughter and not to sit silently.

The ending of a *wayang* in some ways mirrors its opening. In the course of the play the *dalang* metaphorically ties together many "knots" that bind the audience to the story. At the end he "releases" them by revealing the hidden secret of the plot and metaphorically "untying the threads." At some point toward the end of what I would call the performance the audience suddenly gets up and goes home. Meanwhile the musicians continue to play and the *dalang* usually continues to wrap up the story a bit. The *gender* players finish with a closing piece as the audience makes its way home, and the *dalang* carefully puts the puppets one by one into the box and recites more silent *mantras*. The troupe is hosted again, during which time the host gives money to the *dalang*, who gives some or all of it back to the host in polite deference. The host sends ceremonial food and rice to the homes of the performers. Although popular *dalang* are able to make a decent living from performing, their musicians and less popular *wayang* troupes need to supplement their income by other means.

The gradual progression of an evening begins with social interaction and culminates in storytelling and music. The performers and audience are gradually transported deep within the world of the shadow play, the world of the *Mahabharata* or *Ramayana*, where gods, goddesses, demons, and humans interact and traverse kingdoms and spiritual realms. The *wayang* troupe is the vehicle through which the story passes into the modern world of the audience.

CONCLUSION

It is easy to see similarities between different media such as forms of dance, masked dance, (*topeng*), and *wayang*, as the genres draw from and imitate each other. For instance, the dance movements of shadow puppets imitate those of humans, and dancers can imitate puppet movement. The role of the interpreter as intermediary, the way a narrative unfolds and is put together on the spot, the use of oral formulaity, *taksu*, shifting focal points, and even the use of performance space in floor patterns are shared among these media.

One salient, shared feature among genres is the idea of stock characters and the way they are expressed. In the next chapter I introduce you to these character types, which teach us about ideas of social interaction, norms of behavior, and aesthetics. Continuing with the ideas presented in this chapter, I will shift the focus to distinctions between male, female, and androgynous dance styles, concentrating on *legong* and *topeng*. In the listening activities I introduce gong structures that bring characters and dramatic mood to life.

ACTIVITY 4.2 Mahabharata *and* Ramayana

Get familiar with the main story lines of these two epics (see Holt 1967 and others in Resources). Choose one or two episodes within the larger epic and search the library for versions of these. You might find a version from India or a mainland Southeast Asian country such as Thailand, or an Indonesian version from Java or Bali. You will notice that versions vary as the story has been orally transmitted from place to place.

CHAPTER 5

Characterization, Movement, and Gong Structures That Enliven Balinese Theater

In this chapter I discuss aesthetics, character types, and dance movements in *topeng* and *legong*. I also introduce you to some of the main gong structures (colotomic meters) that delineate mood and characterization in theater. After hearing a few of these in isolation we will put the pieces together for you to hear the way these meters and dance and music elements are manipulated in two forms of dance drama: *topeng* (masked) and *kecak* (a vocalized form of *gamelan*). At the end of the chapter I provide a reference and guide to some video viewing.

AESTHETICS AND CHARACTER TYPES: *HALUS* (REFINED) AND *KERAS* (STRONG)

We know that art often imitates life and vice versa. But art is often a vehicle for kinds of behavior that are unacceptable in real life as well. In Balinese theater (shadow play, dance, dance drama, and masked dance drama), two broad character types exist to cover the gamut: *halus*, meaning "refined" (also *manis*, "sweet") and *keras*, meaning "strong," types that exist throughout Balinese and Javanese performing arts. A third type, *kasar*, meaning "coarse, base," an exaggerated form of *keras*, is also opposite to *halus*.

Whether *wayang* puppet or dancer, these types are marked by body type, eye shape and size, vocal timbre and register, face color, clothing, and movement. *Halus* is represented by delicate features, a small body, narrowly shaped eyes, a high lilting voice, and curvaceous, small, fluid movements. The facial color of the puppet, dancer, or mask is white or pale. Figure 5.1 shows the *halus* (refined) character type in dance, *topeng*,

FIGURE 5.1 Halus *character types manifested in dance (left),* topeng *(center), and* wayang *(right). (Drawing by I Dewa Putu Berata.)*

and *wayang*. Notice the similarity in iconography, eye shape, expression, and headdress. The character shows humility by having eyes cast down, avoiding the gaze of another person.

Strong *keras* characters have opposite features: large bodies; large, round eyes; big noses; deep, resonant, and raspy voices; sudden, abrupt, large movements. They may be easily angered and look straight ahead. They are direct, whereas refined characters are indirect. Their facial color is red or some other bright color. Demons have fangs, indicating their bestiality. Numerous characters fit somewhere between these two extremes, covering a spectrum from refined to bawdy, from exquisite to grotesque, from ridiculous to sublime.

Refinement (*halus*) is what everyone strives for, as indirectness, self-control, humility, and polite deference are important aspects of character and social interaction in Bali. They can be seen in business and social negotiations as well as in theatrical performances. As cherished ideals for behavior, they are external representations of inner power and potency. On the other hand, theater allows a temporary release of control as the audience identifies with characters that contradict their held societal values.

MALE, FEMALE, AND ANDROGYNOUS DANCE STYLES

In traditional Balinese theater certain dance styles are strictly male or female. Blurring the two is a third style, known as *bebanci* (androgynous), which is enacted when a male dances a female or effeminate role or vice versa, and when certain dances consciously combine elements of male and female styles. These three—male, female, and *bebanci*—overlap with the *halus/keras* dichotomy: male or female dances can be either refined or strong and coarse. *Bebanci* dances tend to be a combination of the two or to fluctuate between them. In this chapter I look at two types of character dances, one strong and coarse and one refined, in the male masked dance form, *topeng*. The strictly female style (*legong*) on which much of Balinese female dance is based provides comparison.

TOPENG (MASKED DANCE DRAMA)

Masked dancing has been in existence in Bali for at least a millennium. The present form of *topeng* performance developed in the Hindu-Balinese courts of the seventeenth and eighteenth centuries (figures 5.2 and 5.3). The masks themselves acquire a sacred quality and power by being handed down through generations, as do other props such as the sacred daggers (*kris*) worn by the dancer. The art of mask carving is also handed down through family ties, and carvers must be consecrated and trained to deal with the magical powers transferred to the masks.

There are two main types of *topeng* performance: *topeng pajegan* and *topeng panca*. In *topeng pajegan*, a single dancer enacts all parts of the story. This is often done in sacred contexts for ceremonies. The dancer changes masks and characters between each dance or scene. In *topeng panca* several dancers take on numerous roles. The stories are always chosen as a parable for the situation at hand.

The Characters. *Topeng* plays enact semilegendary historical chronicles of Hindu-Balinese kings, their ministers, and high priests, and thus include many characters. The noble characters wear full masks and communicate silently through gesture, *mudra,* and movement. The comic servants translate and interpret for noble characters, or sometimes they may speak for them in Kawi. As in *wayang*, many languages and levels of Balinese are used, a way of acknowledging the hierarchical social roles.

Comic characters, often outrageous caricatures who use slapstick or absurd humor, are the only ones to communicate directly with the audience, through singing and speaking. Good *topeng* performers are known for their versatility, requiring a good singing voice, knowledge of numerous vocal forms and languages, and a vast storehouse of classical poetry from which they draw at any given moment as they spontaneously break into song. A standard pair of comic servant characters are cast according to body type. The elder is stocky and self-important and usually represents the word of his noble master from the past, while the younger is thin and pretends subservience while ridiculing his elder. Their characters are well known, and their routine is expected. There are also endless possibilities for new and unusual comic characters who incorporate images from modern life such as wigs, berets, and hats, doing the latest pop music and dance steps (in the 1980s it was disco, in 2000 it was hip-hop), imitating tourists. A popular character is the male impersonating a coquettish female dancer. The *gamelan* might spontaneously play "Oleg Tambulilingan," the piece that accompanies the flirtatious bumblebee dance by the same name, while the *topeng* dancer does a mock version of the dance. All the clowns discuss local gossip, current events, and political issues. In this way, the history in the legendary stories is evoked in a contemporary setting. Tradition is preserved and recast in light of contemporary politics, with plenty of room for innovation.

Progression of a Topeng *Play.* The stage is set with a curtain at the rear of the stage through which the performers enter. The masked dancer about to enter shakes the curtain, causing much anticipation in the crowd as people try to guess which character it will be. Most theatrical dances open with a pure dance segment. Just as in *wayang* the play begins before the story is introduced, before the actual drama begins in *topeng* there are traditionally four (but nowadays usually two) character dances that have no narrative meaning but simply portray strong and refined character types. These characters have no connection to the particular story. They are meant to "display a mood of wonder and astonishment, as if suddenly wrenched from the distant past into the world of the present, a process characterized by Emigh (1979) as 'ancestral visitation'" (Bandem and deBoer 1995: 49). Dancers have

FIGURE 5.2 Topeng Keras *(strong character). I Ketut Madra, dancer.* *(Photo by Lisa Gold.)*

told me that in order to make the mask come to life they change their facial expressions underneath the mask as they would when dancing without a mask. A good *topeng* dancer can bring a mask to life simply by holding the mask and moving it in his hand.

The first introductory dance often portrays a prime minister, a strong type ("Topeng Keras," CD track 6, figure 5.2) whose actions are broad and sudden, with vigorous shaking of the curtain. A refined dance follows, either a refined prince or king wearing a white mask with a gentle expression ("Topeng Arsa Wijaya," CD track 7, figures 5.1, 5.3), or a dance depicting an old man. The refined king has fluid, gradual move-

FIGURE 5.3 Agem *for refined prince or king character on left* (Topeng Dalem *or* Arsa Wijaya) *and his comic servant gesturing subservience to his right. Anak Agung Bagus Sudarma, dancer on left, and Ida Bagus Gde Mambal, dancer on right. (Photo by Lisa Gold.)*

ments, while the old man moves comically, suddenly moving quickly then stumbling, out of breath, interacting playfully with the audience or picking fictitious lice from his long white wig.

The story begins with the entrance of the two comic servants. Wearing half-masks so they are free to speak, they discuss the plot and particular problem in the story. (This crucial role of interpreter is analogous to the comic servant puppets that have articulated mouths in *wayang*.) The drama is built on a sequence of stock scenes. The dancer-actors follow a general story line but freely embellish, combining memorized poetry and song with improvised dialogue and extended joke scenes interspersed with the action scenes. Often the plot is thin and functions mainly as a vehicle for the humor and other elements. Juxtapositions of the mundane with the spiritual are often used for humor. As discussed in chapter 4, a basic precept of traditional Balinese theater is its blend of sung, memorized portions of old narrative texts, often in archaic languages, with modern improvisatory interpretation.

Free Choreography. The improvisatory format of *topeng* requires an interactive system that enables the dancer-actor to cue the musicians so they know what piece to play and when, at what tempo, and when to stop playing. The choreography is not fixed either; the dancer dictates the sequence of movements following a general framework while leading the musicians to a certain extent. The drummer acts as intermediary, receiving cues from the dancer and giving cues to the musicians. Furthermore, throughout each piece the musicians articulate every movement by interjecting accents known as *angsel* (discussed below).

LEGONG

From the sacred *Sang Hyang Dedari* trance rituals two "secular" genres emerged: *legong* (in the nineteenth century), and *kecak* (in the twentieth century; see below). In *Sang Hyang* (still performed for ritual purposes) two prepubescent girls (*legongs*) sway over incense burners and enter trance while a group of women sing a slow, hypnotic, sacred vocal chant, transforming the girls into heavenly nymph mediums. The entranced girls then dance a complete *legong* performance accompanied by *gamelan palegongan*. The choreography is said to have come centuries ago to a king in a dream as a solution to a village epidemic and pestilence. In the secular version, the dancers are usually three young girls, one of whom plays the role of the *condong* (female attendant to the princess). She also plays the role of the *garuda* bird. The other two are known as the *legongs*.

Many stories are enacted in the *legong keraton* genre. The most frequently performed, known as *lasem*, is related to the Panji tale (see *gambuh*). When Princess Langkesari of Daha is taken in by the vassal to King Lasem, the king falls in love with her and demands her for himself. She rejects him and many ill omens appear, such as a *garuda* bird with whom the king battles.

The *condong* opens the performance with a non-narrative solo dance that ends with her picking up two fans from the stage floor. The two *legongs* enter and the three dance a pure dance trio. At one point the *condong* hands the *legongs* the fans and they go into character as she exits. One girl plays the king and the other the princess who rejects his advances (figure 5.4). The *condong* returns to the stage wearing golden

FIGURE 5.4 *Two* legongs *playing the part of King Lasem (right) and Princess Langkesari (left).* (*Photo by Lisa Gold.*)

wings as she becomes the *garuda* bird and battles with the king (see Resources for videos of *legong*).

Free versus Fixed Choreography. *Topeng* and *legong* illustrate two distinct types of choreography. Unlike the free choreography of *topeng*, in *legong* the dancers memorize a fixed choreography. These two modes of performance derive from the way the drama is put together in each.

In *legong*, the dance and story are continuous. A narrator sits with the *gamelan* and sings and speaks, but the dancers do not stop to speak. A long, exquisitely symmetrical and complex choreographic sequence of movements is set to a precomposed composition that mirrors the movement in its form, elaboration, and melodic drumming. (A complete *legong* performance lasts over forty-five minutes.) The points of articulation are built into the composition so that music and movement are coordinated in a fixed way.

Despite such a fundamental distinction between these two modes of performance, most other parameters of performance are similar. Those parameters have to do with vocabulary of movements (although these differ according to gender and character type), conventions of entrances and exits, floor patterns, and the combination of pure (i.e., noninterpretive) and interpretive (i.e., that tells a story) dance.

ELEMENTS OF DANCE AND MUSIC IN *TOPENG* AND *LEGONG*

In both *topeng* and *legong* the music is crucial in creating the proper mood and level of dramatic tension. Changes in tempo, dynamics, and colotomic meters bring contrasting dramatic situations to life. The drummer is the leader of the ensemble, closely working with the dancer and cueing the musicians. Getting familiar with the dance vocabulary and then the gong structures will help you to distinguish the structures in the subsequent compositions in the book.

Vocabulary of Movements. A multitude of gestures make up the dance vocabulary (see figure 5.10 for a list). These include stationary movements and ways of moving onstage. Some have symbolic meaning (interpretive movements) and some do not (pure movements). Many hand gestures are derived from the Indian *mudras* (figure 1.7). Some, but not all, of these retain their meaning in Bali. Although Balinese dance may appear to be a sequence of movements and repose, the dancer maintains tension throughout the body, displayed by quivering fingers, upturned toes, and eye and head movements, thus giving life even to stationary poses. The floor pattern is always centered and symmetrical, beginning in the downstage center, where traditionally a dancer would enter, through either a curtain or temple gates.

Agem. All three dance styles have a basic stance particular to that style known as *agem*. *Agem* is one of the first positions a dancer will assume to display his or her character type. In the female *agem* the feet are turned out close together with one slightly in front of the other and toes turned up. Most movements, including *agem*, are done symmetri-

FIGURE 5.5 *A refined female heavenly nymph character. Ni Dayu Diastini, dancer. (Photo by Lisa Gold.)*

cally on each side. In "right *agem*" the dancer's weight is on the right leg and she leans to the right; in "left *agem*" everything is reversed. In the male *agem* the feet are wide apart, the shoulders and arms high. Refined and coarse characters are immediately seen in the *agem* of the dancer: refined *agem* is lower to the ground, and the arms and legs are closer to the body; in strong *agem* the legs are straight, indicating arrogance (Dibia 1992: 198), and the arms and stance are wider. Figures 5.5 and 5.6 show contrasting character types in the *agem* position. Please

FIGURE 5.6 *A strong male king character. I Ketut Kodi, dancer.* (*Photo by Lisa Gold.*)

note that the arms in fig. 5.5 are not in the classic agem position. This is seen in fig. 5.9.

While a character is in *agem* position she or he can also have stationary movements. One standard opening movement is called "shaking the curtain." In *topeng* the dancer literally shakes a curtain before

FIGURE 5.7 Condong *maid servant from* legong *shaking the symbolic curtain (a movement called* ngocok langsé*). Dancer from Sanggar Çudamani.* *(Photo by Lisa Gold.)*

opening it and appearing for the first time. In *legong* there is no curtain, yet the dancer shakes a symbolic curtain (figure 5.7). This is followed by "opening the curtain" (figure 5.8). Coarse or strong characters open the curtain suddenly, while refined characters do it gradually.

Once the dancer has "opened the curtain" he or she will step forward and dance in stationary position for a while before gradually traversing forward center stage toward the audience. Again, the speed and directness of these movements is in keeping with the character type. There are numerous possibilities after that, involving various kinds of

FIGURE 5.8 Condong *then opens the symbolic curtain (a movement called mungkah lawang). Dancer from Sanggar Çudamani.* (Photo by Lisa Gold.)

steps for traversing the stage slowly or quickly. Before exiting the dancer always turns away from the audience and performs a special closing sequence of movements with back to the audience, then turns for a final bow, paying homage to the audience with hands together in a gesture of respect before leaving the stage.

An important eye movement is known as *seledet* (figure 5.9). This is a quick movement of the eyes from side to side without turning the head. It is timed to coordinate with certain gongs marking the musical structure. When a teacher teaches dance, she (or he; I will use feminine

FIGURE 5.9 Legong *dancer doing* seledet *eye movement. Dancer from Sanggar Çudamani.* *(Photo by Lisa Gold.)*

here for simplicity) holds her finger up before her student's eyes, moving it for the student to follow with her eyes, reciting mnemonic syllables for the drum, music, dance, and gong strokes. For instance, *seledet* is shortened to "*det,*" and "*pong*" indicates the stroke of the small hanging gong *klentong/kemong.* The teacher stands behind and manipulates the student's arms and body while singing the sequence of movements, indicating the melody and drum pattern, and counting out the steps. In this way the student learns the entire sequence by feel while integrating it with the music. Kinesthetic memory is powerful for musicians in learning a part as well.

Angsel: ***Dance and Music Articulation.*** A crucial articulation of both dance and music is a rhythmic accent or break called *angsel.* It is a point of coordination between drummer and dancer that interrupts the flow of the ongoing music and movement and signals changes and points of transition from one section to another. *Angsels* occur at prescribed points in relation to the gong pattern and follow a predictable sequence, yet their usage differs between *legong* and *topeng.* There are many types of *angsels* in movement and music.

Interpretive dance movements (*gerak maknawi*)

- Shaking the curtain (*ngocok langsé*)
- "Opening the curtain" (*mungkah lawang*), in abstract dances a symbolic movement marking the beginning of a dance
- Sudden movement that cues musicians (a motive of an *angsel*)
- Anger—suddenly pointing with index and middle fingers together
- Looking
- Symbolically adjusting the headdress
- Holding a scarf hanging from costume (a motive often used before the end of a dance, preceding a "long *angsel*")
- A movement originally touching or holding an umbrella or spear, now an abstract movement used for the closing section

Pure dance movements (*gerak murni)*

- *Agem*—main stance of dancer, indicating character type
- Fast stepping from side to side used as a transitional movement
- Quick walking
- A sideways motion where the feet quickly glide apart and together, enabling the dancer to create circular floor patterns
- *Seledet*—eye movement in dance—eyes move quickly from side to side to center, coordinated with the music

FIGURE 5.10 *Dance vocabulary.*

In the free choreography of *topeng*, the dancer initiates *angsels* with certain sudden movements; the drummer responds by playing a signal to the *gamelan*. The drummer therefore must have knowledge of the dance gestures in order to follow. The *ugal* player picks up the cue from the drummer and gestures to the other musicians to *angsel* by raising his elbow and flashing his mallet in the air. In *topeng*, even though the dancer decides when to *angsel*, he must do so at appropriate places in the cycle. Therefore, the dancer must be as familiar with the music as the drummer is with the dance. The musicians are prepared for the *angsel* at any moment, within the understood possible points that it might occur, and they are following the dance themselves. Therefore, even though there is a chain of command from dancer to drummer to *ugal* to the rest of the *gamelan*, the musicians already know they are about to *angsel* before they receive the drum cue. This is the way most cueing in any music occurs: the cues can work only if the musicians expect them! One Javanese teacher compares this to traffic signals: if you see a stop sign on the freeway you are less likely to stop than at an intersection, because it is *out of place.* Here, it is not so much a matter of *where* in the cycle the *angsel* will occur that is unknown, but simply in *which* cycle.

In *legong* and other fixed choreographies, the dancer still appears to be cueing the drummer, even though both dancer and drummer are following a set sequence of *angsel*s. In other words, the rhythmic articulations are coordinated with the movements in a similar way, but both dancer and musicians are following a preset sequence of movements, including *angsels.* The drums and *ceng-ceng* add to the articulation effect tremendously.

Two main types in *topeng* are "short *angsel*" and "long *angsel.*" Both will become clear when you reach activity 5.7 (CD track 6). Short *angsels* are usually only one- or two-beat interruptions and are always syncopated. The long *angsel*s consist of a sequence of events. The dancer cues the drummer with a movement particular to long *angsel.* This occurs immediately following a short *angsel.* The drummer then responds by playing louder, filling in the space following the short *angsel* (otherwise empty). The rest of the musicians know to reenter immediately rather than wait until midway through the cycle as they would in following a short *angsel.* This is immediately followed by a series of swelling dynamics: the melody is continuous, becoming soft and loud several times until the dancer cues the final *angsel,* at which point the musicians break, as in the short one. The music and movement are tightly coordinated: as the dancer bends his knees, swaying from side to side, the music becomes softer. He straightens his knees and raises his arms high, and the music becomes loud. He jerks his hand suddenly, elbow high and bent, and freezes as the music abruptly stops. As he does this, the drummer makes the *plak* stroke with his left hand so that the dancer appears to have made the sound.

Colotomic Meters Delineating Theatrical Situation and Mood. A composer of accompaniment for a dance drama draws from a pool of gong patterns. Some patterns are no more than *ostinatos* (the Western term for short repeating figures), some provide specific dramatic intent, while others allow for expansive lyrical moods. They provide a structural framework for the composer as he or she thinks of the sequence of events in the story and its required musical accompaniment. The composer I Nyoman Windha says he always composes a melody first, then he finds the meter that fits, sometimes altering the meter to fit irregular melodies. In this sense, think of these colotomic meters as models that can be adjusted. It is important to remember the flexibility of musical elements in composition, and that it is the totality of musical elements that results in creating a particular mood.

The way a particular melodic cycle is marked or punctuated by gongs of various sizes, along with the length of the cycle (i.e., the number of beats per gong), affects the dramatic mood and degree of tension. These contribute to the pacing of a scene or bringing characters to life. For example, in a short, two-beat gong cycle, a high density of gong strokes creates tension; an eight-beat gong cycle with a syncopated pattern marked by subsidiary gongs creates forward motion; and a 128-beat cycle allows for more melodic development in the space between the gong strokes and is usually more fitting for relaxed situations and refined characters. These gong patterns are also played in pieces that have no dramatic function, yet their dramatic associations remain because they are so ingrained. The colotomic meter of a piece is usually named after the genre or melody with which it is most closely associated, even when it has been transferred to another genre or melody. This holds true for patterns in other instruments as well. A drummer might, for instance, convey a certain drum pattern to another drummer by simply saying "Jagul," or a *reyong* player will refer to a certain pattern as "Baris," each the name of a piece with which that pattern is most closely associated. In this sense, patterns have *identity*. That primary association is a *model* for other pieces like it. This fits into the idea of formulaity discussed in chapter 4.

This section presents theater usage as a way for you to get familiar with some gong patterns and their primary associations. The gong patterns in figure 5.11 make up some of the building blocks of instrumental music that you will be studying in chapter 6 as well. Please note that some of the colotomic meters originate in *gambuh* and *legong*, where a *kempur* (abbreviated as *P*, or *pur*) is used instead of the larger gong. In meters originating in *gamelan gong*, however, the large gong (abbreviated as *G*) is used in addition to *kempur*, which becomes a subsidiary gong.

The gong patterns are lined up together in the figure (out of their musical context) for you to see their relationship and relative length, from cycles of two to sixteen beats. Numerous longer cycles (up to 512 beats long) appear mainly in instrumental and temple music, but I am focusing on the shorter ones that are most prevalent in theater. (Activ-

Cycles in other types of composition extend to 512 beats per gong. Drum patterns also distinguish each form. See "Topeng Arsa Wijaya" below, "Sinom Ladrang" (ch. 6) for two examples, and Gold 2001 for tabuh lalambatan and semar pagulingan.

Suggestion: Make a circle diagram for each colotomic meter here, marking the final *G* or *P* at 12 o'clock and filling in the other symbols. Recite the forms, beginning on the final beat of each cycle.

Symbol	Instrument	Mnemonic syllable
tuk	*kempli/kajar*	(*tuk,* as in "took")
P	*kempur*	(*pur,* as in "poor," deep, with rolled *r*)
G	*gong*	(*gong,* or *sir,* deep, with rolled *r*)
T	*klentong*	(*tong,* sharp attack; also called *kemong*)
n	*kelenang*	(*nang,* high pitch, slightly sharp attack)

Batel

gongs:	*n*	*T*	*n*	*P*
		tuk		*tuk*
beats:		1		2

Omang

gongs:	*n*	*T*	*n*	*P*
	tuk	*tuk*	*tuk*	*tuk*
beats:	1	2	3	4

Bapang

gongs:		*P*		*T*		*P*		*G*
	tuk	*tuk*	*tuk*	*tuk*	*tuk*	*tuk*	*tuk*	*tuk*
beats:	1	2	3	4	5	6	7	8

Gabor longgor

gongs:								*T*								*P*
	tuk	*tuk*	*tuk*	*tuk*	*tuk*	*tuk*	*tuk*	*tuk*	*tuk*	*tuk*	*tuk*	*tuk*	*tuk*	*tuk*	*tuk*	*tuk*
beats:	1	2	3	4	5	6	7	8	9	10	11	12	13	14	15	16

Gegaboran

gongs:				*P*				*T*				*P*				*G*
	tuk	*tuk*	*tuk*	*tuk*	*tuk*	*tuk*	*tuk*	*tuk*	*tuk*	*tuk*	*tuk*	*tuk*	*tuk*	*tuk*	*tuk*	*tuk*
beats:	1	2	3	4	5	6	7	8	9	10	11	12	13	14	15	16

Gilak

gongs:				*G*	*P*		*P*	*G*
	tuk	*tuk*	*tuk*	*tuk*	*tuk*	*tuk*	*tuk*	*tuk*
beats:	1	2	3	4	5	6	7	8

(*Kalé* = *gilak* form, but *pokok* consists of one repeated note.)

FIGURE 5.11 *Some colotomic meters (gong patterns) used in theater and dance.*

ities 5.1 to 5.5 exemplify the structures in figure 5.11.) In each, the abbreviations for the syllables used for reciting the patterns are given with the *kempli* pulse so you can recite the patterns with the CD. It will help if you review activities 2.3 and 2.4 before going over figure 5.11.

Before doing the activities notice in figure 5.11 that some gong patterns are identical but are elongated versions of others (twice as long). The single exception to this is the *gilak* colotomic meter. Sometimes the elongated form is called *longgor,* as in *gabor longgor* on the chart. In the following activities each gong's entrance is staggered for the demonstration so you can hear individual parts. This would not be done in performance.

Batel. *Batel,* meaning "agitated," is used for scenes of intense action such as fight scenes. It has the shortest gong cycle, functioning as an ostinato, originating in *gambuh* but used in *kebyar* and other ensembles. The gongs and drums provide a steady framework. The *ceng-ceng* (delicate plate of cymbals) reinforces the drum patterns. The *suling* (flute) improvises freely in a fashion typical of *batel,* juxtaposed with the rhythmic grid provided by the other instruments.

This seemingly simple pattern contains two levels of ostinato. The *kajar* maintains the pulse (say *tuk tuk*); the *kempur* strikes every two of these (say *pur*); the higher-pitched *klentong* plays on alternate *kajar* strokes (say *tong*); then the highest-pitched horizontal gong, the *kelenang,* strikes in between each *kajar* stroke, providing another level of offbeat (say *nang*).

ACTIVITY 5.1 *Batel (CD track 30).*

With three classmates, each of you "say" one of the gong parts, keeping a steady pulse and using the syllables provided. Follow along with the time counter below.

gongs:	*nang*	*tong* *tuk*	*nang*	*pur* *tuk*
Beats:		1		2

00:00 kajar *alone*
00:04 kempur *added*
00:10 *klentong plays slow offbeat, alternates with the* kempur

00:24	kelenang *plays fast offbeat, alternates with* kajar
00:35	suling *enters*
1:22	*drums and* ceng-ceng *enter with an* angsel, *preceded by a second* suling
1:34	angsel
1:55–57	angsel

Omang. CD track 31 accompanies the *barong* dance drama on *gamelan palegongan*. It has no *reyong* but delicate, static *gangsa kotekan* that is articulated with *angsels*. The piece fits the playful and energetic nature of the *barong* character (see video guide below). The pattern consists of four *kajar* beats marked by a *kempur*, divided in half by the *klentong*, with the *kelenang* playing on the offbeat, like a longer form of *batel*, a bit more relaxed.

ACTIVITY 5.2 Omang *for* barong *(CD track 31)*

Try saying the syllables with three other classmates and compare its feeling to batel.

gongs:	*nang*	*tong*	*nang*	*pur*
	tuk	*tuk*	*tuk*	*tuk*
Beats:	1	2	3	4

Bapang. This eight-beat cycle can have a lively, intense feeling. The excerpt on CD track 32 has *reyong* and *gangsas* playing *kotekan* with *angsels*.

ACTIVITY 5.3 Bapang *(CD track 32)*

Say the gong pattern as you listen.

gongs:		*pur*		*tong*		*pur*		*gong*
	tuk	*tuk*	*tuk*	*tuk*	*tuk*	*tuk*	*tuk*	*tuk*
Beats:	1	2	3	4	5	6	7	8

Gabor Longgor. The word *longgor,* though not taken from English, indicates a long form of a pattern. *Longgor* implies elongation and relaxation. The piece "Jauk Manis," used here to demonstrate this gong pattern, accompanies a sweet (*manis)* type of a demonic mask dance of the same name, hence the longer cycle. There is no *reyong* in this piece, just *gangsas* playing a delicate *kotekan* with *angsel*s (this piece is also played on CD tracks 21–23 to demonstrate *kotekan telu,* played on a higher pitch level. The cycle is sixteen beats long, marked by the *kempur* and divided by the *klentong*. The *kelenang* plays on the offbeats.

ACTIVITY 5.4 Gabor longgor *(CD track 33)*
Compare this to batel *and* omang *and you will see that it is an elongated form of these, with quite a different feel. Follow along with the pattern on Figure 5.11.*

Gilak. In contrast to the patterns of evenly distributed gongs you heard thus far, *gilak* is one of the few asymmetrical, hence syncopated, colotomic meters. It has widespread use, providing forward motion for a dancer or procession, as the *kempur* pulls toward the gong.

Activity 5.5 introduces the gong pattern in isolation. In activity 5.6 you can hear the pattern in *balaganjur* (processional *gamelan*) and then in activity 5.7 in "Topeng Keras." *Gilak* becomes recontextualized as a form called *kalé* (CD track 7, 3:46), used to accompany intense action in *topeng* where the *pokok* is reduced to a single repeating note. This should give you an idea of how a single pattern can be used in a number of musical contexts.

ACTIVITY 5.5 Gilak *(CD track 34)*
Try to get the pattern in your system by clapping or stomping your feet. Gilak *uses both large gongs, the lower female* wadon, *striking on beat 8, and the higher, male* lanang, *striking midway through the cycle. To feel the syncopation of the* kempur *that plays on beats 5 and 7, sing through the gong*

structure. Then try tapping the tuks *with your foot, saying the gongs and clapping the* purs.

gongs:				*gong*	*pur*		*pur*	*gong*
	tuk	*tuk*	*tuk*	*tuk*	*tuk*	*tuk*	*tuk*	*tuk*
Beats:	1	2	3	4	5	6	7	8

Gamelan Balaganjur. The processional *gamelan* piece heard in CD track 9 is the prototype for the *gilak* meter as it moves people in processions with *gamelan balaganjur.* See if you can keep track of each level of ostinato in this piece. Here it is played in a much slower tempo than the previous example; its tempo is flexible and adjusts to the processing crowd. *Gamelan balaganjur* takes the idea of group cooperation to its maximum: in order for the musicians to be able to walk while playing, each plays only a single gong, drum, or pair of crash cymbals. One or two people support the gong pole on their shoulders, and the two drummers hang their drums on straps around their necks. You will get a sense of the difficulty in interlocking with only one pitch to play if you review the *reyong* demonstration from chapter 3 and try to beat out only one of the pitches in any given pattern. It takes tremendous skill and group cooperation to do this up to tempo.

ACTIVITY 5.6 Gilak *pattern in* gamelan balaganjur *(CD track 9)*

The gong and kempur *pattern is* gilak *(as in activity 5.5). Two smaller gongs play a syncopated ostinato moving at the rate of the* kempli, *or timekeeper. Four* reyong *players, each holding a single kettle, play rapid interlocking figuration that when sounded together forms a single melodic line. Two drummers playing large drums with mallets play an introduction and then play intermittently, cueing tempo and dynamic changes and the entrance of the cymbals (*ceng-ceng kopyak, *playing in interlocking pairs). Notice the contrast of this to the delicate interlocking gong-chimes. After listening to this excerpt listen to the interlocking precision and tight group coordination in a contemporary* balaganjur *composition, CD track 10 (see Bakan 1999 for* kreasi balaganjur*).*

LISTENING TO TWO *TOPENG* PIECES

Each of the four *topeng* dances that precede the drama in a *topeng* play is accompanied by a piece that consists of a single colotomic meter. The next two activities focus on two contrasting *topeng* dances: "Topeng Keras" and "Topeng Arsa Wijaya."

ACTIVITY 5.7 *"Topeng Keras"*

This strong masked character type has a high-level energy conveyed by gilak. *This listening activity has three stages.*

(A) First get familiar with two layers of the melody with the gongs in the demonstration in CD track 35. The excerpt begins with the pokok *played once on the pair of* jublag. *The* panyacah *enter with the filled-in melody. Both parts are notated below. Although the gong cycle is eight* kempli *beats long, the melody lasts two cycles (sixteen* kempli *beats). Try to count the sixteen beats of the complete melody, saying the* gilak *pattern and learning the melody by listening to it numerous times. This will allow you to get comfortable reading the cipher notation. Review the key of symbols for gongs (*tuk *is on every beat, but some are omitted here for clarity of the overall pattern). Remember that the cycle begins on the gong 1.*

key: Male Gong ○ Female Gong 1̂ Kempli ⁺ Kempur ˘

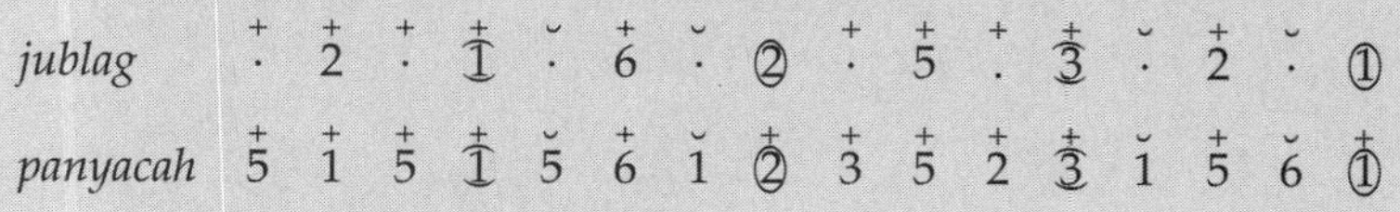

	+	+	+	+	˘	+	˘		+	+	+	+	˘	+	˘	
jublag	·	2	·	1̂	·	6	·	②	·	5	.	3̂	·	2	·	①
	+	+	+	+	˘	+	˘	+	+	+	+	+	˘	+	˘	+
panyacah	5	1	5	1̂	5	6	1	②	3	5	2	3̂	1	5	6	①

(B) To help you hear some other layers, review CD track 27 (activity 3.8, reyong *interlocking for this piece). Gongs and* ugal *enter at 1:14. In this excerpt the* ugal *plays a slight variant of the melody, yet the contour (i.e., melodic shape) is retained, enough to satisfy Balinese musicians and dancers. In this sense, there is a generic idea of a piece (such as this one), with permutations of details.*

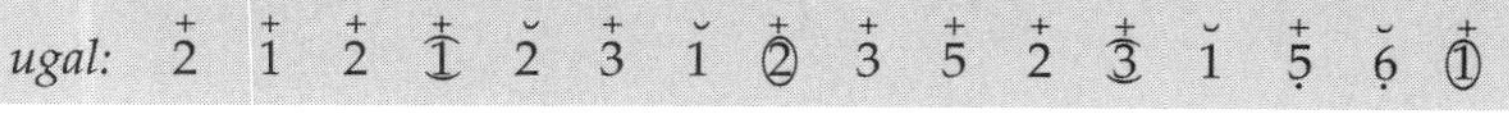

	+	+	+	+	˘	+	˘	+	+	+	+	+	˘	+	˘	+
ugal:	2	1	2	1̂	2	3	1	②	3	5	2	3̂	1	5̣	6̣	①

(C) Performance Version of "Topeng Keras" (CD track 6)

Now you are ready to listen to an excerpt of a performance version of the piece with all the parts (CD track 6). In the previous listening activity the ugal *plays a slight variant of the melody. In this example the standard melody is the one that stands out. Remember that the dot under the note indicates that note is played in the low octave. This melody, played on* ugal *and* gangsas, *exploits the two-octave range by playing the low pitch 5̣:*

5̣ 1 5̣ 1̮ 5̣̆ 6̣ 1̆ ② 3 5 2 3̮ 1̆ 5̣ 6̣̆ ①

Once the full ensemble enters, the ugal *switches to its embellishing role and the* panyacah *and* gangsas *play the melody that is audible. Due to the limited one-octave range of the* panyacah *you will hear a high pitch 5 rather than the low one that the* ugal *plays. Even with reversed contour such as this, the melodic integrity remains constant and identifiable. The drum plays an introduction, followed by the* ugal *entering alone (0:13). All the other instruments enter with an* angsel *shortly before the gong (0:17). Notice the sound of the drum played with mallets.*

After each angsel *the* ugal *enters alone, followed by the rest of the* gamelan *midway through the cycle. Follow the time code for the* angsels. *Notice the dynamic contrasts and drum activity preceding and following each* angsel. *Try to imagine the* topeng *dancer cueing each* angsel.

Short angsels occur at: 0:28, 0:34, 0:52, 1:09, 1:15, 1:38, and 1:44.

The last short angsel *is immediately followed by a long* angsel *sequence. Notice that the drumming remains active following this* angsel, *cueing the rest of the ensemble for the long* angsel. *Remember, the long angsel has this sequence: an increase and decrease in dynamics spanning several cycles, ending at 2:06 with a short* angsel. *This excerpt ends with a fade-out, but in performance the piece continues much longer, then ends with a slight slowing of tempo to a final gong.*

In contrast, one of the four introductory character dances, *"Topeng Arsa Wijaya,"* named after a king by that name (also called *"Topeng Dalem"*), accompanies a dance for a refined prince or king character (figure 5.3). The form of this piece (*tabuh dua,* "form of two") has a long gong cycle played at a slow tempo, fitting for the slow, stately, refined movements of this character. *Tabuh dua* is manifest differently with each genre. This version is typical of *topeng* and other theatrical performance, where the "two" refers to the number of times the *kempur* strikes per gong cycle. There are thirty-two *pokok* tones (notated below) per gong. Every four *pokok* tones there is a *jegogan* (lowest metallophone) stroke. The *kempur* strikes on beats 4 and 28, and the big gong is on beat 32. When the tempo is slow, the *kempli* time marker strikes on every other *pokok* tone, including the gong tone. Later (2:16 in CD track 7) the tempo increases and the *kempli* doubles so that it plays on every beat.

ACTIVITY 5.8 *"Topeng Arsa Wijaya," followed by dramatic excerpt (CD track 7)*

Before doing the listening activity, just listen to the piece once to get the feeling of its expansive, stately form (especially in relation to the previous examples).

Unlike "Topeng Keras," the piece opens with an ugal *introduction, followed by drum, cueing the rest of the musicians to enter with an* angsel *(00:06). The* gangsa *section plays the main melody along with the ugal. At 00:20 the* reyong *enters with the open-closed* byong-jet *strokes.*

A brief ugal *solo interlude is followed by entrance of the full ensemble. This entire opening section, called a* kawitan *("beginning"); is often a compressed form of the main body of the piece to follow. At 00:27 the* gangsas *reenter and play the final four beats of the main body of the piece (the* pangawak*).*

At 00:41 the pangawak *begins, marked by the gong. Try to follow along with the transcription below. As a guide, you can count eight* ceng-ceng *strokes between each* pokok *tone. You will hear other layers of melody playing in between the notated tones.*

Cipher transcription of "Topeng Arsa Wijaya" (CD track 7)

key: gong ○ *kempli* ⁺ *kempur* ˘ *jegogan* ˆ *klentong* —

Ugal *solo introduction leads into* Kawitan

Pokok *of* Kawitan *(Beginning, played by* gangsas, *punctuated by low instruments)*

							+^								+^								+^
·	6	·	6	·	3	·	5	·	5	·	3	·	2	·	5	·	5	·	3	·	5	·	2

00:20 Ugal *interlude*

00:26 gangsas *enter with* angsel *and play an elaboration of the last four beats of* pangawak:

	+	·	+
6	3	1	⑥

Pangawak *(main body) (begins at 00:39 and repeats at 2:14 and 2:56)*

	+		★		+		+^
1̇	6	2	5	5	2	3	5
	+		+^		+		+^ —
5	3	5	2	5	3	2	5
	+		+^		+		+^ a
5	2	3	5	5	3	5	2
	+		★		+		+^
6	6	6	3	6	3	1̇	⑥

The gangsas *elaborate by playing the main* pokok *tone and its upper neighbor. When the tempo increases (beginning at the gong at 2:15) the* gangsas *switch to playing* kotekan *by dividing up the melody pitches:* polos *players play the* pokok *tone on the beat and* sangsih *players play the upper neighbor tone off the beat* (kotekan norot). *The* reyong *players also use* norot. *If you listen closely you will hear the* panyacah *filling in the* pokok *by playing neighbor tones evenly spaced between each* pokok *tone. Also notice the* angsel *inserted on the last line after the third high 6 each time.*

3:20 tempo slows and gangsas *return to pivoting between both notes.*

3:27 break: ugal *leads into the ending of the piece;* gangsas *enter on pitch 3, preceding it with 3353, and then they play the final four* pokok *tones, identical to the end of the* kawitan.

Following the refined dance, the play proper begins. In the small fragment on CD track 7, an immediate transition leads into another *topeng* piece (from 3:46), used as background filler to provide dramatic tension for the entrance of a coarse character. It consists of a single repeated note played by all metallophones. During the dialogue (or monologue) the only instruments playing are those that provide the colotomic framework, *suling* and low metallophones. When the dancer is not speaking, the *gangsas* and *reyong* enter. At this point there is some action occurring onstage. This colotomic meter is called *kalé* and has the same colotomic pattern as "Topeng Keras" (*gilak,* figure 5.11). The tension level is heightened by the repetition of a single pitch (pitch 3). The *reyong* play a kind of figuration that creates a rapid, ascending stepwise run of four notes.

ACTIVITY 5.9 *Accompaniment for dialogue, action, or drama (CD track 7 from 3:46).*

Listen to the interaction between the comic servant's vocal cues, the drum cues, and the rest of the ensemble's response. The sequence is as follows:

3:51 suling *with colotomic instruments*
4:02 *comic servant speaks, interludes without* gangsas, *full ensemble,* angsel *at 4:10*
4:11 suling, *comic servant speaks, interludes without* gangsas, *dancer cues* gamelan
4:35 *full ensemble,* angsel *at 4:43, interlude, full ensemble, comic servant sings*
5:12 suling *and gongs*
5:21 *dancer cues all musicians to enter*
5:32 *slows to end*

The colotomic meters I have covered support a variety of forms of drama. *Kecak*, the final example, uses the meters in a vocalized form of *gamelan* in which the actors provide their own musical accompaniment.

KECAK

In some versions of *Sang Hyang* (see *legong*, above), once a state of trance is reached, a male *cak* chorus would chant interlocking parts to maintain the link with the spirits inhabiting the bodies of the girls, chanting the syllable *cak* (pronounced "chak"). Using this as a basis for a new kind of performance, a vocalized form of *gamelan* was created. Said to have been influenced by some of the "cultural tourists" living in Bali during the 1920s and 1930s, a dance drama enacting the *Ramayana* was created. It became known as *kecak*, or the "Monkey Chant," because of the major role the monkey armies play in the *Ramayana*. It is now a popular form of entertainment for Balinese and tourists that has become a medium for experimental choreographers.

Kecak is performed by a group of men, sometimes numbering in the hundreds, representing monkey armies, and a few male and female principal dancers. Seated in concentric circles, the "monkeys" provide the interlocking *cak* over a sung melodic line led by a narrator (CD tracks 36 and 37). It is always performed outdoors at night around a fire, often in a forest setting outside a temple. The dancers might swing from Banyan tree vines or use other natural props such as bonfires and hot coals. In the course of an entire *Kecak* performance many melodies and gong structures are used to accompany distinct scenes and choreographies.

ACTIVITY 5.10 Kecak *demonstration and piece*

CD tracks 36 and 37 are examples of kecak *interlocking over two melodies. This is an activity that you and your classmates can do. Appoint a group leader to give the cues. Consult videos for movement (see "Video Resource," below).*

Track 36 begins with an eight-beat pokok *(main melody) and "gong" cycle, then switches to a four-beat melody, then a two-beat cycle with no melody.*

00:00 *the* kempli *part, a steady beat* "pung pung pung pung . . ."

00:05 *sir* (= *gong*) *count the eight-beat cycle*

00:17 "cak cak cak cak cak" *(leads into the first pattern. Patterns are presented individually)*

00:36 *cue* ("chi") *given to stop the "cak"*
00:43 *second pattern (like first but offset to the offbeat so that it interlocks with first pattern)*
1:03 *cue ("chi") given to stop "cak"*
1:06 *third pattern*
1:18 *cue given to* cak *loudly*
1:25 *cue ("chi") given to stop "cak"*
1:36 *all patterns interlocking together*
1:51 *cue given to* cak *loudly*
1:58 *cue ("chi") given to stop "cak"*
2:03 *melody begins on gong* (sir)

5̣	1	1	5̣	5̣	3̣	3̣	⑤
yang	*ngir*	*yang*	*ngur*	*yang*	*nger*	*yang*	*sir*

2:13 cak *interlocking added to melody*

Cues given to get loud, soft, stop, and start

2:48 new four-beat ostinato melody

1	5̣	1	5̣
yang	*ngur*	*yang*	*sir*

3:30 *new two-beat gong cycle (*bok *sir)*
4:04 *ending pattern:* cak cak byok sir!

CD track 37 has a sixteen-beat melody. Listen for the cues given to start and stop the pattern, and to get soft and loud.

VIDEO RESOURCE AND ACTIVITY 5.11

In addition to these activities you may want to view the JVC Anthology of World Music and Dance, *volume 9,* Bali, *in which you can immediately see the relationship between music and its dramatic function. Begin by viewing the* Baris *dance, a*

A battle between Rangda and *Barong,* which has been simplified for tourist audiences as a battle between good and evil. This staged daytime performance has none of the supernatural aura that nighttime ritual performances have.

Zero counter with first appearance of caption.

Key: G = gong; T = tong; J = jegogan; P = kempur

Characters
Matah Gede = the evil witch
Minister
sisyas = disciples of the witch, Matah Gede
panasar = two comic male servants
Kalika = a demon
garuda = mythical bird from *legong*
Rangda = the major witch character, embodies evil
Barong = protector of the village, mythical creature danced by two dancers
note the minister's use of pointing gesture at 16:43

Time	Activity in drama	Description, level of intensity	Beats per cycle	Gong pattern (colotomic meter) and notes
Beginning	Overture	medium level	8	*gilak*
1:21	Entrance of disciples	movement	8	*bapang,* fast tempo then slows to end.
1:55	Talking	stylized vocal style from *gambuh*		silent
2:18	Matah Gede enters	short for entrance tempo slows	8	*bapang,* 4-beat melody fits twice into gong cycle, once to *tong,* once to gong
2:39		long cycle as background for speech	16	*gegaboran: tong gong* alternate, *jegogan* on 4, 12 serve colotomic function
3:36	Transformation	transition		*(penarik):* accelerating *kajar* strokes with *gangsa* repeated notes then silent
4:28	Matah Gede hits disciples Matah Gede exits speaking	high level of tension, fast beat	2 3	*batel,* wild *suling,* no melodic metallophones, ends at 6:05
6:30		lyrical	64	*Pangawak, gender rambat* intro; *kajar* and drum join; *tong* on 32, 60; J every 8; *gangsas* play *norot kotekan*

FIGURE 5.12 Calonarang *video* (JVC Anthology of World Music and Dance vol. 9, Bali)

(continued)

Time	Activity in drama	Description, level of intensity	Beats per cycle	Gong pattern (colotomic meter) and notes
7:52	*Sisyas* spread disease	fast	8	J . T . J . G .
8:22	*Panasar* (male servants) enter (or) comic servants	fast	8	fast, 2-note ostinato, alternates with 4-note, note the delicate drumming and *kajar* playing drum patterns
9:10	cut to the minister's entrance (male role played by female)	refined character, so longer, slower	8	*bapang* (like "Bapang selisir," ch. 6)
				tong gong, different melody, *kajar* keeps beat
				gangsa patterned kotekan then *norot* at 10:14
10:36	prime minister (man)	coarser character, so fast and loud	8	Back to two-beat ostinato, as for *panasar;* note the *angsels; gender rambat* part can be heard during breaks
11:29	dialogue, then exeunt			
			2	*batel*
12:14	villagers enter to bury child		8	*gilak* melody, should be ...GP.PG, but just ...G... G yet melody is eight beats long and has a *gilak* function and feel
12:47	digging grave		2	*batel,* no melody, free *suling*
14:88	fighting with Kalika;	*angsels*	2	*batel* continues
	minister and *panasar* enter	colotomy continues under speech		*gangsas* enter with two-beat ostinato at 17:06, extended form of *batel* to four-beat
17:23	*garuda* (from *legong*)	fight	2	*batel,* PTPG; *angsels* articulate the fight
17:52	Rangda enters	dialogue, then fight (18:57)	2	*kale*
19:34	*barong* enters	*barong* melody, medium level	4	*omang barong,* T G, *gangsa* part alternates between plain pivoting between two notes and *kotekan*
20:58	Ending	ending piece "Tabuh gari" (1st section only of multimovement piece traditionally used to signify ending of a performance)		introduction played on *gender rambat*

1. Try to notice gong cycles—length and colotomic meter. (Use your chart from figure 5.12 to identify patterns). How does this influence mood, characterization and drama?
2. What other musical, dance, or other elements contribute to portraying the drama (such as tempo, dynamics, melody, *kotekan* or no *kotekan,* etc.)?
3. Make a visual representation of this performance that shows the way music is used to shape the drama.

FIGURE 5.12 (*Continued*)

male martial dance, to see the relationship between drum and dance and the way that angsels *work in the type of free choreography discussed in the "Topeng Keras" example.*

Also view the Calonarang *performance on this video. Please note that this video is a staged performance, simplified for tourist audiences and devoid of the magic and supernatural aura with which a "traditional"* Calonarang *is imbued. The gamelan sekaha Tirtha Sari play on a* gamelan palegongan *(note the delicate timbre), which is different from the one on your CD, so some things will sound different, and they even play slightly different versions of some of the gong patterns. You will, however, get a sense of how the gong patterns function in a real dramatic sequence. You can find all of the colotomic meters demonstrated here used in other pieces in the Calonarang video, where they are strung together in a continuous dance drama. In figure 5.12 I chart the gong patterns with the action in the video example. See Resources for other videos.*

ACTIVITY 5.12 *Construct your own dance drama accompaniment*

After viewing the calonarang *video, refer to figure 5.11 and create your own dance drama using the colotomic meters on the chart. You may invent your own story or draw from any that you like (I have had students do this with* Mahabharata *episodes,* The Lord of the Rings, *and fairy tales). First delineate the character types and classify them according to Balinese classification* (halus, keras, *male, female). Then make a story board (scene sequence chart) and choose the musical accompaniment, making a score of the gong patterns with text describing the action onstage. Be sure to include comic interpreter characters and state what languages are being translated. Through this intermediary, try to weave together past and present ideas and aesthetics. For instance, you might use a Shakespeare play while interweaving current political events.*

CONCLUSION

My *wayang* teachers express concern that modern audiences are losing patience with the slow pacing and careful character portrayals of traditional theater. They continually say that, in their day, teaching and philosophy were paramount, and that the youth of today watch too much TV and film and are only interested in the joke and battle scenes. Although an exaggeration, this has nevertheless led to truncated performances and loss. Yet, despite changes, the function of performance remains relevant.

Through the integration of stories, music, dance, and theater, people are linked to past and present situations. Stories told in *wayang kulit* concern the mythological world of the Hindu pantheon. The *legong* and *gambuh* tales evoke Hindu Java. The stories told in *topeng* from the world of historical Balinese legend are one step closer to the present reality. My teachers see these as representing parallel worlds in the Balinese present. They say that dancers and musicians can easily traverse these worlds through performance, bringing the audience with them, playing the past in the present. This is largely done through modern-day intermediaries who translate and paraphrase, bringing new meaning and relevance to old themes.

In this chapter I introduced the idea of individual colotomic meters, ranging from two to 512 beats long, with distinctive metric patterns made by the various punctuating gongs within the cycle and by drum patterns. Some pieces are self-contained gong cycles, consisting of a single, repeating metric framework, as in "Topeng Keras" and in pieces fulfilling functional, dramatic categories. There is much more to composition, however. When musicians compose new music they draw on these earlier, dramatic gong frameworks and other musical materials and juxtapose them in longer compositions (see Tenzer 2000 for detailed analyses of this process). In chapter 6 you will learn about what I am calling "large-scale form," meaning the sequence of movements that make up a composition. As the most significant twentieth-century development in Balinese music, *gong kebyar* serves as a bridge between the enduring themes presented thus far and the extremely vibrant musical culture of today.

CHAPTER 6

Large-Scale Form in *Gong Kebyar* and Its Antecedents

The three themes of this book converge in *gong kebyar*. Cooperative interaction enables ensemble musicians to achieve phenomenal levels of competence and group cohesion. The source material for much *kebyar* composition lies in the primacy of theatrical references with which most music is linked. And finally, tradition encompasses innovation, as new compositions refer to past practices in the contemporary music scene. Beginning with large-scale musical form that predates that of *kebyar*, in this chapter I take a brief look at ways this earlier sense of form is modified in *kebyar*.

Inherent in Balinese composition is the idea of contrasting movements, or sections. In earlier, "classical" composition, there is a clear progression from one movement to the next. But *kebyar* form is predicated on the idea of sudden and extreme juxtaposition, even within each movement. *Kebyar* textures, asymmetrical gong cycles, and an increasing linearity play a large part in defining its form, as you will learn in this chapter.

"CLASSICAL" TRIPARTITE FORM

I will use the term "classical" to denote pieces, forms, and ensembles from court and temple that predate and influence *kebyar*. One typical classical form—the one I focus on here—stems from *gambuh* and *gong gede lalambatan* (slow temple music); it is conceived to have a tripartite form. I say "conceived" because, although this may be the case for many pieces, it is not so for all. Because the concept of threes is all-important in Balinese ideology, a tripartite structure is often imposed on ways of thinking. The examples from chapter 1 ("Thinking in Threes") are linked to fundamental Hindu belief systems such as the *trimurti* (Hindu trinity of deities, Brahma, Siwa (Shiva) and Wisnu (Vishnu)) and the *triloka* (three worlds: upper, middle, and lower).

Three Contrasting Movements. The classical three-movement form of a musical composition is likened to the human body: its opening section (*kawitan*) is considered to be the head, its middle section (*pangawak*) the torso or "main body," and the final section (*pangecet*) the feet. A progression in mood and pacing are predictable in this form:

- The **head** of the piece (*kawitan*) is short and condensed and played at a brisk tempo. All of the *gangsas* play the *pokok* rather than *kotekan* as the main themes of the piece are clearly presented. As in "Topeng Arsa Wijaya" (CD track 7), the *kawitan* may be a compression of the *pangawak* to follow and always has a regular pulse, beginning fast and slowing down to settle in the *pangawak* tempo. Not all pieces have a *kawitan* in this classical sense. The *kawitan* may be substituted with some other short opening piece. It is still considered to fit into the tripartite way of thinking about the unfolding of the composition, however.
- The **main body** (*pangawak*) has the longest gong cycle of a piece, permitting melodic and thematic development, and it is played at a slow, stately tempo. It may be repeated several times, sometimes with a long pause between repetitions. A lengthy, fixed sequence of drum patterns common to all *pangawak* within a type of *gamelan*'s repertoire identifies the form to any listener. The drumming, number of beats in the cycle, and colotomic meter are "regular" in this sense. Musicians refer to the *pangawak* form according to its *gamelan* of origin, e.g., a *gambuh pangawak,* or one of many *lalambatan pangawak* forms.
- The final section, the **feet** (*pangecet*), has a fast tempo and a shorter gong cycle in relation to the main body. Often thematic and melodic material from the main body is heard in a condensed form. Its tempo increases after several repetitions, building to a climax before the piece ends. You listened to the final section of "Jaya Semara" at the end of chapter 3. The *pangecet* cycle may consist of an irregular number of beats, or even two alternating gong cycles.

Gineman: Metrically Free Preludes. Preceding, and in some cases instead of, a *kawitan* is a *gineman*, a metrically free prelude, with no fixed pulse, played by the soloist of the ensemble. *Gineman* are not really considered part of the tripartite form described above but are free standing, lyrical preludes that provide the proper mood and, to a certain extent, allow for individual expression and improvisation. *Gineman* follow a melodic path that musicians learn, but precise timing and ornamentation are spontaneous. The soloist (or group of soloists) explores the mode and feeling of the piece that follows, inserting long, breathy pauses. Later you will hear the way *gineman* are transformed in *kebyar* composition.

ACTIVITY 6.1 Gineman

Listen to the following excerpts to hear that there is no strict pulse, pokok, *or gong framework. Space does not permit complete gineman examples here.*

In CD track 3 (excerpt of a lalambatan gineman*) hear the way the* trompong *(gong-chime soloist; figure 2.11), accompanied by* suling *and* rebab, *melodically prepares for subsequent* jegogan *punctuating pitches. In a full performance the melody starts in the low register and works its way up to the high end of the instrument and then back down again. Try to plot the contour of the* trompong *melody in this excerpt.*

In CD track 8 (gamelan gambuh gineman, *00:00–52*) *the* gineman *is played on a group of* gambuh suling *(large bamboo vertical flutes), and in CD track 29* (gamelan gender wayang gineman, *shortened here, 00:00–1:35*) *on a* gender wayang *quartet. In both instances, the solo group has less room for individual variation. The timing and feeling are left to the spontaneity of the musicians, whose phrases breathe and move together as a group.*

LISTENING TO AN ENTIRE PIECE: THE TRIPARTITE FORM IN "SINOM LADRANG"

To acquaint you with the form, I have selected a well-known piece, "Sinom Ladrang." Musicians always like to try something new, and the following listening guide presents a variant of the classical form in that piece. Because a more standard rendition—that is, with *gineman, kawi-*

tan, pangawak, pangecet—is easily available (see Nonesuch H 72046 in Resources), I have put on CD track 38 a version in which a composer, I Nyoman Windha, has adapted this classical piece by choosing to fulfill the three-movement form with a piece preceding the main body (*pangawak*). "Bapang Selisir" is an independent piece that can be attached to other pieces and here takes the place of *kawitan*. The *gineman* is not played here. Windha said he did this to create contrast in mood: "Bapang Selisir" has a light, energetic mood, while the rest of "Sinom Ladrang" is a bit more serious and sweet. In this performance, the *gamelan* leader, I Dewa Putu Berata, (a former student of Windha's at STSI, now a prominent composer and director of Çudamani) chose to use Windha's rendition. This is a good example of the flexibility of a "piece" and the transmission of ideas as materials are manipulated. A complete performance of "Bapang Selisir," originating in *gambuh*, has its own *pangawak* and functions as dance accompaniment. Here only the first section is borrowed. "Sinom Ladrang" is a classical *semar pagulingan* piece, purely an instrumental composition with no dramatic intent other than the delicate, sweet mood, originally reserved for the king's bedchamber.

Semar pagulingan pieces were originally intended to be played on a seven-tone (*saih pitu*) *gamelan* that has the capacity to play in several modes. This particular rendition of the piece is played on such a *gamelan*, allowing for two contrasting modes: *selisir* and *tembung* (review activity 2.2). Befitting its name, "Bapang Selisir" is composed within the *selisir* scale, using the pitches 1 2 3 5 6. The piece that it precedes, "Sinom Ladrang," begins in *selisir* but briefly modulates to *tembung*, using the pitches 4 5 6 1 2. In the *pangawak* of "Sinom Ladrang" the juxtaposition of pitch 3 with pitch 4 is sometimes used for color, to "sweeten the line."

You can apply what you have learned about the instrument types and the stratified texture in *gong kebyar* to this type of *gamelan*. The instruments themselves are smaller and more delicate and sweet in timbre than those of *kebyar*, and there are a few other differences (you might want to make note of these on your figure 2.5). The medium-sized gong, *kempur*, is played instead of the large gong, and the *kajar* replaces the *kempli* as timekeeper, which in the main body plays a composite of the two drum patterns. The drums are smaller and sweeter in timbre than those of *kebyar* and there is no *reyong*. Instead of *ugal* (large metallophone leader), the *trompong* player (gong-chime soloist) is the melodic leader, playing all introductory passages (Figure 6.1). He embellishes the *pokok* throughout the performance. In a sense he improvises, but with clear constraints to follow the composed melodic line. Especially in the *pangecet* he alters the rhythm and adds ornaments.

FIGURE 6.1 *Faculty musicians at STSI. I Nyoman Windha plays* ugal, *I Komang Astita plays* trompong. *(Photo by Lisa Gold.)*

Follow the three guides for each section of the piece, remembering that it was necessary to cut several repetitions of each section for this CD, although the performance length is flexible. I provide cipher notation for the basic melody (*pokok)* played on the *panyacah* and the *jublag*. The *trompong* plays a more ornate version of this melody throughout.

ACTIVITY 6.2 "Bapang Selisir" *(opening section to* "Sinom Ladrang"*)*

This simple opening section consists of an eight-beat melody in the bapang *meter. Unlike* bapang *for* gong kebyar *noted in figure 5.11,* semar pagulingan *ensembles have* kempur *fulfilling the function of the gong. The* klentong *strikes halfway through the cycle. The symbols show the gong punctuation above the numbers. The piece begins with the solo* trompong *playing a brief, two-note introduction, then a statement of the eight-beat melody. See if you can follow the* pokok, *using the cipher notation below. The eight-beat melody is repeated a number of times.*

Pokok of "Bapang Selisir" *(CD track 38, 00:00–1:49)*

key: *Kempur* O *klentong* — *kajar* +

Trompong introduction 2 · $\bar{3}$ ⑤

+	+	+	+	+	+	+	+
3	6	3	$\bar{2}$	3	6	3	⑤

Using the listening guide in figure 6.3, listen for the repetitions of the *pokok* melody and the changes that occur. Even though the main melodic idea of this brief first "movement" in the tripartite form is so short and simple, there is immense variety and musical interest owing to *angsels*, dynamic contrasts, and sequential diversions, giving it shape. Here are some suggestions:

- Start at the *kempur* strokes noted in the far right column of figure 6.3. *Kempur* is both the first and the last note of the piece. The time code should help you follow along.
- Note the dynamic shifts; cycles are played softly and loudly. Between loud cycle 9 and the return to cycle 1, listen for a sequential transitional passage made up of five eight-beat phrases.
- Listen for the way the drum prepares each *angsel* with a short syncopated pattern.
- Finally, listen for the *empat* (4) *kotekan*, played throughout by the *gangsa*. It has become a classic, often used in beginning lessons. The full staff notation for the repeating portion (i.e., without the transitional passage) is given in figure 6.2.

The *pangawak* (CD track 38, 1:49–4:58) has a long, convoluted, yet catchy melody that lasts 128 beats. When you listen to it, try to follow along with the cipher notation below. Here are some things to notice about *pangawak* in general and in this piece in particular:

- As in the previous movement, the *trompong* plays the lead melody (i.e., in the foreground of the texture, elaborating the *pokok*), reinforced by the *jublag* and *panyacah*, and punctuated by the *jegogan* at the end of each sixteen-beat grouping (note time markings).

FIGURE 6.2 *Staff notation for "Bapang Selisir" including* gangsa kotekan.

- The *gangsas* play *empat* (4) *kotekan* that surrounds the *pokok.*
- The *kajar* plays the drum composite rather than the regular pulse. This is typical of *pangawak* as is the melodious drumming style of the smaller-sized drums of this ensemble.
- The *pangawak* is slow and expansive, with a flexible tempo. Try to notice as the tempo speeds up and slows down, especially at phrase endings. This flexible tempo is similar to the music of the neighboring island of Java, which may have influenced this style, although the particulars of tempo changes are quite different. The dynamics also have an ebb and flow. You will note in the guide in figure 6.4 that the dynamic changes are more or less the same with each repetition.
- The number of *pangawak* repetitions is flexible. In this performance the *pangawak* is played twice before moving into the *pangecet* (note time markings).

Repetition	Dynamics	Activity	Time of *kempur*
1	soft; *trompong* alone	continuous	00:07
2	soft; full ensemble	continuous	00:13
3 & 4	loud	continuous	00:19 & :24
5	soft (*trompong* alone, *gangsas* enter later in cycle)	*angsel* at end	00:29
6 & 7	soft	continuous	00:35 & :40
8	loud	continuous	00: 45
9	loud	*angsel* twice	00:50
---------	loud	louder, transition begins	00:56
---------	loud	transition ends with *angsel*	1:14; 1:19
1	soft	return to main *pokok*	1:21
Here I have cut to a later portion that speeds up			
2–4	soft	building in intensity, faster	1:26 etc.
5	loud	*angsel*	1:38
4	slows down, leading into *pangawak,* which begins at the *kempur*		1:49

FIGURE 6.3 *"Bapang Selisir" listening guide*

- When the melody moves to pitch 4, notice the temporary mode change (line 4). Prepare by first singing *selisir* then *tembung* (see above).
- To facilitate reading this cipher notation, remember that the *kempur* (gong) strikes at the *end* of the last line (circled), at 1:49, 3:21, and 4:55. The *jegogan* strike at the end of every line, indicated by the time markings (the first is at 2:01). The *pokok* changes to · 2 · ① the last time through as a transition into the *pangecet.*

Moving into the final section, the *pangecet,* both tempo and pulse change (CD track 38, 4:55): the tempo increases while the pulse also doubles. This tempo increase is typical of *pangecet.* You can hear this by

Key: kempur ◯ klentong — jegogan ˆ kajar (plays drum pattern)

Pokok of *pangawak* (main body)	Line #	1st time	2nd time	Notes
Kempur at end of "Bapang Selisir" ①		1:49		
· · · 2 · · · 1 2 1 6̣ 1 · 2 · 1̂	1	2:01	3:33	*selisir* mode
· · · 1 · 2 1 6̣ · 1 · 2 · 3 2 1̂	2	2:12	3:46	*selisir* mode
· · · 2 · · · 1 · 2 1 6̣ · 1 · 2̂	3	2:23	3:57	*selisir* mode (louder)
· 4 · 5 · 4 · 5 · · · 6 · 1̇ 6 5̂̄	4	2:35	4:08	*tembung* mode
· · · 6 · · · 5 6 5 3 6 5 3 2 1̂	5	2:46	4:20	*tembung* mode
· · · 1 2 3 1 2 · · · 1 · 2 1̣ 6̣̂	6	2:57	4:32	*selisir* mode (louder)
· · · 6̣ 1 2 · 1 · 5̣ 6̣ 1 · 6̣ · 5̣̂	7	3:09	4:43	*selisir* mode (louder)
· 6̣ · 1 · 2 · 3 5 3 2 1 · 6̣ 2 ①	8	3:21		*selisir* mode
end of line leading into *pangecet* · 2 · ①		4:55		*pokok* substitution

FIGURE 6.4 *Pangawak* "Sinom Ladrang," pokok *and listening guide (CD track 38, 1:49–4:55)*

focusing on the *kajar*, which switches to a regular pulse (4:55). The *pangecet* can be counted according to the *kajar* pulses, of which there are eight per line.

Remember, the part notated in figure 6.5 is the basic melody (*pokok*) played on the *panyacah* and the *jublag*. The *trompong* plays a more ornate version of this melody. Notice how syncopated the melody is here,

Pokok of *pangecet* (final section)	Line #	1st time	2nd time	3rd time	Notes
Kempur at end of *pangawak* ①		4:55			
· +· 2 +1 6̣ +1 2 +· 1 +· 2 +1 6̣ +1 2 +·̂	1	5:00	5:44	6:26	low register
1 · 2 1 6̣ 1 2 1 4 5 · 4 5 2 4 5̂	2	5:06	5:49	6:31	
· · · · 6 5 4 5 4 2 · 4 5 6 1̇ 6̂	3	5:11	5:54	6:35	
· 1̇ 6 1̇ · 2̇ · 1̇ 6 5 · 4 5 2 4 5̂	4	5:16	5:58	6:40	
· · 6 1̇ 6 5 4 · 5 · 6 1̇ 6 5 4 ·̂	5	5:20	6:03	6:44	high register
5 · 6 1̇ 6 5 4 5 6 1̇ . 6 5 4 2 1̂	6	5:25	6:08	6:49	
· · · · 2 1 6̣ 1 . 6̣ 5̣ 6̣ 1 2 4 2̂	7	5:30	6:12	6:53	return to low
· · · · 4 2 1 2 1 6̣ · 1 5̣ 6̣ 1 6̣̂	8	5:35	6:17	6:59 slows	
· 1 2 1 · 6̣ · 5̣ 6̣ 1 · 6̣ 1 2 6̣ ①	9	5:40	6:21 faster	7:07	

FIGURE 6.5 *Pangecet* "Sinom Ladrang," pokok *and listening guide (CD track 38, 4:58)*

often juxtaposed to the low-pitched *jegogan* punctuation, which always falls on strong beats. This syncopation is typical of *pangecet*. This *pangecet* is in *tembung* mode. Melodically, the *pangecet* is made up of two contrasting thematic groups, a low and a high segment, totaling seventy-two beats. The low part of the melody lasts four lines, followed by two lines in the high register and three in which the melody works its way back to the beginning *kempur* tone. Like the *pangawak*, the *pangecet* may be repeated any number of times. Here it is played three times (note time markings at the end of each line).

INNOVATIONS IN FORM AND TEXTURE IN *KEBYAR KREASI BARU* (NEW CREATIONS)

In the early twentieth century, as *gong kebyar* emerged, several significant changes came about in the musical scene. "Classical" pieces, adhering to established forms and textures, are not attributed to individual composers. Now, however, individual composers began to be credited for their compositions. Dances and pieces free of narrative content were created. A new freedom liberated composers from preexisting musical norms, allowing them to explore new ways of composing. Nevertheless, the "classical" tripartite form of earlier works remained as an underlying template on which new forms were superimposed.

I have chosen two contrasting *kebyar* pieces that demonstrate some innovations and developments in composition. "Jaya Semara," the early *kebyar*-style piece you have already heard in chapters 2 and 3, has an innovative texture that broke away from the smooth, stratified model of *semar pagulingan*, *palegongan*, and *gamelan gong*. In "Jagra Parwata" you will hear ways this style matured and expanded later in the twentieth century. These pieces are both *kreasi baru* ("new creations"), a term adapted from English ("creation") and Indonesian ("new") and used for *kebyar* compositions from the early twentieth century to the present.

As a category of composition, *kreasi baru* is now well established and completely absorbed into Balinese tradition. By this I mean that these pieces are widely accepted by audiences to the point where they may be played in conjunction with ceremonies to fulfill important functions. The innovations within *kebyar* composition that diverge from its predecessors have gradually become accepted as the new "tradition." Compositions have been developing tremendously since the early days of *kreasi baru*, yet audiences are so familiar with them that they know more or less what to expect and how to evaluate their merits. They have become "classical" in their own right. New performance contexts (and mass media) allow large, island-wide audiences to hear what is being composed in other areas than their own, and to become wildly popular. The *kebyar* style has influenced most forms of *gamelan*, which now have *kebyar*-style *kreasi* in their repertoire in addition to those traditional to the ensemble.

Form *in Kebyar: Cyclicity and Linearity.* *Kebyar* composition demonstrates a free-flowing artistic exchange at the very core of Balinese creation. As is the case with most new art forms in Bali, when music was and is composed for the *gong kebyar* ensemble, elements of earlier forms and ensembles are "borrowed" and inserted into pieces in new ways. When transferred into different *gamelan* these traits sound new while still being familiar and therefore acceptable to the Balinese ear. Musical elements such as gong structures and figuration have specific connotations because they are closely associated with those of theater, dance, or ritual. Furthermore, once a new piece is performed it is considered to be in the public domain, and any other composer is free to borrow elements from it to incorporate in new pieces.

Form in *kebyar* compositions owes much to theatrical accompaniment (*legong*, for instance), in which several repeating melodic cycles of differing lengths with contrasting colotomic meters are strung together (unlike the clear progression of the classical instrumental tripartite form above). In this sense, the piece has, in addition to its internal cyclical repetitions, a linearity as it progresses and changes through time. The entirety of "the piece" (i.e., its large-scale form) includes all of the repeating cycles, transitions between them, and juxtaposed melodies, levels of density, dynamics, rhythm, and tempi. While there is an element of linearity in the tripartite instrumental pieces, it is more pronounced in these theatrical, multisectional works.

Within such works the shorter melodies function as ostinatos, whereas longer cycles have developed melodies that comprise several phrases. Cyclic sections may be connected with transitional passages that do not repeat. Or a transition is simply made by switching from one cycle to another at the gong after a cue is given, either by dancers, actors, or by the drummer, such as in the *topeng* excerpt from the previous chapter. Sometimes the precise progression from one type of colotomic meter to the next is predetermined, such as in the dance pieces of the *legong* genre, where dramatic function determines the colotomic meter. The form in most *kebyar* pieces are conceived in this way, even when devoid of drama.

When cycles with contrasting gong patterns, tempi, and textures are strung together, moods are juxtaposed. While this occurs in theater accompaniment of the court genres to some extent, in *kebyar* composers take this idea of juxtaposition to new levels and extremes by composing purely instrumental (i.e., nonprogrammatic) compositions full of juxtapositions. Furthermore, *kebyar* compositions have become increasingly linear (as discussed below). This will be explored in the two *kebyar kreasi baru* discussed below.

New Textures. The most obvious aspect of the *kreasi baru* that differs from court-style compositions is the texture. We heard in court-style pieces such as "Sinom Ladrang" the stratified texture in which all instruments play together: the lower the register, the slower its pace. While this sometimes occurs in *kebyar*, additionally, each subset of the ensemble is given its chance to shine by playing passages alone. Here, for the first time, timbral distinctions were brought out. For the sake of simplicity I will call these passages "solos" even though it is the entire group of *gangsas*, four *reyong* players, two drummers, *suling* group, and so forth that is playing. It is not part of this style to have a single musician take a solo; even the so-called solos are done in groups. One purpose of these group solo passages is to display virtuosity. This ability for musicians to play incredibly fast with absolute precision in interlocking and damping, to execute sudden dynamic and tempo shifts, and to play as a single entity, seems to take on superhuman proportions in Bali and results from intense and extensive rehearsals. This is especially apparent in *gong kebyar*.

Another element of this new freedom in texture is an expansion of orchestration possibilities that highlights contrasts in register and timbre. Composers use unconventional instrument combinations and new devices such as antiphonal contrasts. You will hear these new textural elements in "Jaya Semara" and "Jagra Parwata."

Kebyar *Passages: A Display of* Gaya. All *kebyar* pieces contain at least one section known as a *kebyar* passage (some contain several). This all-important type of musical passage has no regular pulse or *kempli*, yet the entire ensemble moves as one by following an intermittent, flexible, implicit pulse, and by following the gestures of the *ugal* player. In *kebyar* passages the entire ensemble plays a highly syncopated melody together almost in unison. This consists of brief, sporadic melodic gestures strung together with spaces in between. The complete statement of each melody is played on the *gangsas* (led by *ugal*) and reinforced by the low instruments that emphasize the final note of each melodic unit. The *reyong* divide the *gangsa* melody between the two pairs of players. The melodic fragments themselves can be exceedingly difficult to play on *gangsa*, even for highly competent musicians, because they often require the musician's hand to leap over keys, sometimes from one end of the instrument to the other as low and high pitches are quickly juxtaposed. Many techniques are interspersed such as staccato repeated, accelerating notes, or sliding the mallet along the keys from one end of the *gangsa* to the other without damping, allowing the notes to blur together in a flourish at phrase endings.

The *ugal* player plays a critical role in keeping everyone together by gesturing with his elbow and flashing his mallet in the air before striking the keys, working in close tandem with the lead drummer. Absolute precision is required in these passages. This is greatly enhanced by group *gaya* (charismatic gesture; see chapter 3).

Kebyar-*Style* Gineman: Gegenderan. Some early *kebyar kreasi baru* open with many short, sporadic musical gestures attached to one another by short transitional passages—sort of a *kebyar* transformation of the earlier *gineman*. Some musicians call this a *kebyar-style gineman.* These *kebyar gineman* display compositional innovation, technical virtuosity, and the timbre of the particular ensemble (CD track 11).

In later pieces the *gineman* is usually played by the metallophones ("Jagra Parwata," CD track 39). It consists of brief periods of *kotekan* and unison strokes separated by pauses, allowing the tuning "waves" to resonate. The unison segments draw on the music of *gender wayang* and the *gender* parts in *legong* preludes, which employ phrases such as the gradual acceleration of a repeated single note, beginning with the key damped and gradually allowing it to resonate (activity 6.1). Because these sections emulate the music of the *gender* and are played on *gangsas*, of the *gender* family themselves, they are referred to in *kebyar* as the *gegenderan* ("in the manner of *gender*").

"JAYA SEMARA" ("VICTORIOUS DIVINE LOVE/LOVE DEITY")

The piece "Jaya Semara" (CD track 11) was composed in 1964 by one of Bali's most renowned composers, I Wayan Beratha. The piece is actually a reworking of an earlier piece composed in the 1930s, so it is a good example of the early *kebyar* style. It has become a standard that all musicians know how to play. In chapters 2 and 3 you studied parts of this piece. Now we will put the components together.

The first section is an alternation of energetic, virtuosic solos. If you compare this opening to "Sinom Ladrang" you will notice a marked departure from the smooth fluidity and continuity of texture and gesture, as "Jaya Semara" boldly announces its jagged difference from norms of court styles. While the bulk of the piece consists of these sporadic, juxtaposed musical gestures, there is nevertheless continuity owing to compositional design, interrelated musical motives, and pitch material. As you can see in figure 6.6, at 2:31 there is a move into the *pangecet*. Here the *gangsas* and *reyong* alternate antiphonally in dynamics. When the *gangsas* are loud they play the leaping *kotekan* (*nyog-cag*). When the *rey-*

Kebyar gineman
00 *kebyar:* full ensemble in unison
00:07 *reyong*
00:09 *kebyar:* full ensemble in unison
00:15 drum interlocking briefly interjects
00:17 *kebyar:* full ensemble in unison
00:30 *reyong*
gangsa gegenderan
00:34 *reyong* solo no. 1
00:48 *kebyar:* full ensemble in unison
00:56 *gangsa* interlocking
00:58 *kebyar:* full ensemble in unison
1:04 melodic *gangsa* interlocking
1:08 *ceng-ceng*
1:11 *reyong* solo no. 2
1:23 brief *kebyar:* full ensemble
1:26 continuation of *reyong* solo no. 2; drum, *ceng-ceng, kempur,* gong interjects
1:43 *ugal* intro to transition section played by full ensemble
1:52 *panyacah, jublag,* and *jegogan* transition section; full ensemble enters, *angsels*
2:05 extended drum solo

Pangecet (*bapang* colotomic meter: *pur, tong, pur, gong*)
2:31 full ensemble, gangsas alternate between two kinds of *kotekan*
(1) neighbor tone, loud *reyong* interlocking
2:53 (2) leaping, gangsas louder than *reyong*
3:13 (1) neighbor tone, loud *reyong* interlocking
3:33 (2) leaping, gangsas louder than *reyong*
3:54 (1) neighbor tone, ending with full ensemble getting loud together

Kebyar ending
4:13 *angsel* leading into final *kebyar,* syncopated, full ensemble
4:29 *gangsa* interlocking
4:31 *kebyar* full ensemble ending in a loud flourish

FIGURE 6.6 *"Jaya Semara" listening guide (CD track 11)*

ong is loud the *gangsas* play the neighbor-tone *kotekan* (*norot*) as you heard in isolation in chapter 3. The piece ends with a brief, climactic *kebyar* ending that recalls its opening.

The relationship between form and texture is at play here, as form is secondary to texture, the main focus of "Jaya Semara." Nevertheless, the *kebyar* ending gives the piece a tripartite form, albeit drastically different in shape from the court model and devoid of a true *pangawak* (main body).

TRANSFORMATION OF FORM AND OTHER INNOVATIONS

Kreasi since the 1980s have become increasingly long, changing shape and departing from the "Jaya Semara" models. In contrast to "Jaya Semara," which is under five minutes long, many pieces last at least twenty minutes. The tripartite structure has expanded to four or five sections. Each section has become extended, sometimes to the point where it is not repeated, with extensive transitional passages, leading toward a new kind of linear composition that moves away from cyclicity (see Vitale 1996 and Tenzer 2000).

Musical borrowing from ensembles from the Old historical category that do not have the constraints of binary gong structures is another innovation of *kreasi.* By drawing from these unconventional *gamelan,* asymmetrical cycles of varying lengths and new kinds of rhythmic emphases and figuration devices were made available. One device that became popular was to have a final *gegambangan* (in the style of the sacred xylophone ensemble, *gamelan gambang*) section, with idiosyncratic meters and *kotekan* ("Jagra Parwata," below). This takes the place of the final *pangecet.*

The late 1980s forward have seen other innovations as well. One is the use of pitches that are external to the *selisir* tuning of the *gamelan.* This is done through the use of instruments without fixed pitch, such as *rebab* and *suling,* during interludes (such as CD track 39 at 5:23). New orchestration was also used, such as contrasting the high register *kantilan* with the low *jublag* (00:43 and 4:29 in "Jagra Parwata"). In the 1980s some composers began adding a vocal part, often in choral singing that emulates music of Java or incorporates forms of Balinese sacred chant.

GONG KEBYAR COMPETITIONS AT THE BALI ARTS FESTIVAL

The twentieth century saw an expansion of contextual possibilities with the appreciation of "art for art's sake" in secular performances on proscenium stages outside of the ceremonial contexts. The Bali Art Center (Werdi Budaya), which opened in 1976, is a frequent venue for the students and faculty of the government performing arts institutions, for tourist performance such as a weekly *kecak* performance, and, most importantly, for the annual Bali Arts Festival (Pesta Kesenian Bali, hereafter referred to as PKB, instigated in 1979).

The PKB is a competition and exhibition of *gamelan*, dancers, and artisans from throughout the island. The *gamelan* festival, the major focus of the PKB, promotes a competitive atmosphere, regional pride, and appreciation of music among *gamelan* groups and audience members. One *gamelan* from each of the nine districts of Bali is chosen to represent the district in "playoffs" prior to the festival, which narrow the competition to two groups. For an audience of some six to eight thousand people and a panel of judges, these performances are held in a "battle of the bands" format, with a *gamelan* group on either side of an enormous stage and the audience in stadium seating. The two groups alternate playing pieces, some purely instrumental compositions and some with dance. Repertoire must fit into the categories of required pieces established annually by an official committee, and most pieces are newly composed for the occasion. More esoteric genres are also featured and draw smaller audiences in more intimate settings.

The culmination of the festival, and the most popular events for Balinese audiences, are the *sendratari* and *drama gong* dance-drama performances. *Sendratari,* an acronym of *seni,* drama, and *tari* ("art," "drama," and "dance", respectively) is a huge spectacle involving hundreds of dancers, musicians, and a narrator. *Drama gong* is a dance-drama in which the actors speak, accompanied by *gamelan gong.* Aspects of these forms depart from traditional Balinese theater and dance. Complete epic narratives are played out in encapsulated form. Further, their choreographies, *gamelan* pieces, and script are set. This leaves little room for improvisation (see Picard 1990). Another important feature of these performances that differs from traditional theater is the use of the proscenium stage. Remember that in traditional settings the audience surrounds the performance area on three sides. The impact on choreography has been that a linear use of the stage space is required so that the dancers face the audience. Familiar stories are used, however, as many narratives have been adapted to both *sendratari* and *drama gong* formats.

The sheer magnitude and scope of these PKB performances has influenced the nature of the audience's response. You can hear the crowd response several times during the performance of the piece "Jagra Parwata" (CD track 39). Not only does the audience respond to all nuances, showing appreciation for well-executed passages, good interpretation, and innovative composition and choreography, but it also expresses vehement regionalism. It is truly like a sports event, as fans cheer the performers representing their district of Bali, while sometimes trying to distract those of the other side. The regional pride reinforces community bonding on the local level, even when it is expressed in such a "nontraditional" context. Unlike a sporting event, however, the audience is required to have a certain degree of knowledge and understanding of the performing arts in order to know how to evaluate them and to respond as they do.

"Jagra Parwata" ("Awakening of the Mountain"; CD track 39) was composed in 1991 by the renowned composer and STSI faculty member I Nyoman Windha, for the group from Munduk, Buleleng, North Bali, to play at the PKB, where this performance was recorded. It has the overall form *gineman, gegenderan* (2:26), *bapang* (4:29), *gegambangan* (6:12). When I asked Windha about the form of the piece, he explained that although there are four major sections and many transitional passages, with each section full of new musical ideas, the old tripartite structure is still there: the *kebyar*-style *gineman* opens the piece; the *gegenderan* and *bapang* sections combined are analogous to a *pangawak;* and the final *gegambangan* section functions as a *pangecet*. Windha says that the head is still a head, the body still a body, and the feet are still feet, while the individual features differ from those of other pieces, just as individual features of every human being are unique. The piece normally runs around fifteen minutes, but I have had to drastically cut it here (see Vital Records 402 in Resources for the complete recording).

Try to notice the changes in mood from one section of the piece to another. Not only does Windha fill the piece with innovative meters and other musical ideas, but he also artfully shapes the entire composition. The audience responds to these innovations because they are new and different, as well as to those aspects that are familiar. Notice the wild audience response as the tempo relaxes while the mood builds at the beginning of the final *gegambangan* section. Some highlights of each section are noted in the guide in figure 6.7.

ACTIVITY 6.3 *A comparison of forms*

To understand the huge impact of gong kebyar *on the music scene in the early twentieth century, after you have studied the listening guides carefully, immerse yourself first in the courtly sound world of* "Sinom Ladrang" *by listening to the piece several times (CD track 38). Then listen to* "Jaya Semara" *(CD track 11). List your immediate responses to the new textures and*

(1) Gineman

gangsas play delicate *kotekan* in sporadic gestures (note audience response); *jublag* and *jegogan* punctuate; *gangsas* play in unison.

0:28 *reyong,* short solo, gong at end; pause

0:38 a regular beat is established; the *gangsas, kempli,* and *jublag* play melody; *gangsas* play *kotekan;* ends with *gong*

0:43 *kantilans* featured with *jublag* melody (audience response)

0:52 all *gangsas* reenter

1:06 sporadic, unison, and *kotekan*

1:23 regular pulse

1:28 *reyong* and drums enter: *kebyar* section in unison

1:37 drums only (audience response)

1:45 *kebyar* section in unison (full ensemble)

1:57 *reyong* solo

(2) Gegenderan

2:26 *suling* (flute); syncopated *jublag* melody playing with groupings of three against four

2:40 *reyong* enters briefly

2:44 *gangsas* enter; *reyong* drops out

2:52 gong; melody repeats (as in 2:26), now with *gangsas* added to fluid *jublag/suling* melody; *reyong* interjects briefly, repeats

3:17 gong; second melody (the *gegenderan* section repeats at 3:58 but here it is cut)

3:58 gong; 1st transition; *reyong* interjections; *kebyar* (audience response approaching *bapang*)

(3) Bapang Section

4:29 *kantilan* (high *gangsas*) play melody with syncopated *jublag* (note the contrast of very low *jublag* paired with very high *gangsas*); *reyong* alternates between percussive role and melodic role; note the thirty-two-beat, elongated *bapang* colotomic meter *(pur, tong, pur, gong);* percussive *reyong, ceng-ceng,* and drums work as a unit (*ocak-ocakan;* see chapter 3) with melody

4:40 *reyong kotekan*

4:51 repeat of cycle (like 4:29)

5:14 second *kebyar* transition; tempo slows

5:23 *suling* (flute) plays a seven-tone *pelog* melody while only the *kempli, jegogan,* and gongs play sparsely; note the sixteen-beat, elongated *bapang* colotomic meter *(pur, tong, pur, gong)*

5:52 *kebyar* and *kotekan,* full ensemble

6:07 repeat of entire *bapang* section (several repeats, ending with transitional material that is cut here, leading into final section)

(4) Gegambangan

6:12 relaxed tempo and mood

6:18 new, singable melody on *jublag* and *suling; gangsas* embellish; *reyong* plays percussively, alternating with *kotekan* (audience response); several other segments with many *kotekan* types; repetitions of *pangecet* (cut here)

7:17 slows, ends with final gong (audience response)

FIGURE 6.7 "Jagra Parwata" *listening guide (CD track 39)*

juxtapositions. What are some of kebyar's *innovations that you hear in this piece? What colotomic meters (gong patterns) are carried over from the theatrical genres you have studied?*

Now do this comparison between "Jaya Semara" *and* "Jagra Parwata" *(CD track 39). What sorts of developments in* kebyar *large-scale form do you hear? What new orchestration and other devices does I Nyoman Windha use? What gong patterns are used and what is their effect? How does he achieve this expansion of the sound world of* gamelan? *(Hint: for each comparison note the contrasts in orchestration, tempo, dynamics, register, rhythm, and pitch).*

KREASI BARU TRENDS AT THE DAWN OF THE TWENTY-FIRST CENTURY

In "Jagra Parwata" you heard the seven-tone section that Windha achieved by using the *suling* and *rebab*. Breaking out of the *selisir* tuning constraints became so popular that musicians started reviving the old seven-tone gamelan *semar pagulingan* and forging new experimental *gamelan*.

One type combines the five-tone *selisir* with seven-tone tuning. The *gangsa* key sequence consists of a low octave that is in *selisir* and an upper octave of seven tones, totaling twelve keys. It is known as *gamelan semara dana,* or *semarandana* (*semara* and *dahana* combined), fittingly named after a tale of the love deities, Semara and his consort, Ratih, whose smoke unite as one when they are cremated. Taking on the name *semara* references earlier ensembles such as *semar pagulingan* and the other *gamelan* of the "gods of the four quarters" (chapter 4). This type of *gamelan* has become quite popular, offering composers a chance for experimentation with modulation while retaining the large sound of *gamelan gong kebyar*. The ensembles have the capacity to play *semar pagulingan* and *legong* repertoire, *kebyar* standards, and even *angklung* pieces in the *slendro* tuning, as well as cutting-edge experimental music. This latter category is not yet fully accepted into "tradition" to the extent that the *kebyar kreasi* are. Although these works draw on classical materials, they musically recontextualize and alter them significantly. The *gamelan semarandana* excerpt on CD track 40 is an example of such a

Only a brief excerpt of "Pengastungkara" is played here. Its form does not fit into the old tripartite model but does emulate some standard dance piece genres. Try to hear the juxtaposition of modes.

00:00	*kawitan* (dancers enter) in *tembung* mode; *gangsas* play *gegenderan*
00:05	*reyong* solo
00:12	full ensemble
00:16	beginning of mode change
00:20	moves to *slendro,* slow opening section (dancers are assembled onstage)
1:42	modulation to *tembung*
3:06	transition
3:34	*pangecet* (moves into *selisir* tuning)

FIGURE 6.8 "Pengastukara" *listening guide (CD track 40)*

composition. The entire performance of "Pengastungkara" ("We Give Blessing") is 8:37 minutes long.

Composed by I Dewa Ketut Alit (figure 2.11) in 2000, "Pengastungkara" is an exploration in modulation (changing mode). You will probably recognize some familiar techniques and gestures while hearing that the pitches used are quite different from those of *kebyar*. The piece accompanies a group offering dance at the beginning of a performance and follows some conventions inherent in that genre.

Kontemporer. In contrast to *kreasi baru,* and a more extreme departure from acceptable norms than pieces like "Pengastukara," is a category of composition called *kontemporer* (from the English word "contemporary"), established in the early 1980s. Composed primarily by faculty and students at national music academies throughout Indonesia, these compositions diverge drastically from traditional molds while linking Balinese composers with their counterparts in other areas both within and outside Indonesia. Since students from many Indonesian provinces study together at these institutions, these compositions are often cross-pollinations of musical styles from many Indonesian cultures, exhibiting national pride and solidarity with the modern Indonesian self, while looking beyond Indonesia to Western and other foreign models.

I Nyoman Windha has composed many works that fall somewhere between *kontemporer* and *kreasi,* such as a piece performed at a large festival in Denpasar, Bali, in 2001 with the theme of "Unity in Diversity," Indonesia's motto. Windha describes his intention in composing a piece that shows the importance of acknowledging all of Indonesia's diverse ethnicities. In his composition Windha incorporates musical elements of Sumatra and Sunda, among others.

In more extreme cases *kontemporer* composers make new instruments, sometimes from everyday objects such as brooms and stones, or imitate sounds from nature by squeaking plastic bags to sound like birdcalls. They also find new ways of playing old instruments, such as bowing a *gender*, or putting water in a gong-chime kettle. While such pieces are not played in traditional settings, they often reflect or comment on daily life and the symbolism of religious practices.

Theater and dance, too, are seeing experimentation. New forms of *wayang*, for instance, use electric lighting, large screens, and multiple *dalangs*. Some combine dance with *wayang*. Significantly, even though the works and contexts diverge in extreme ways from the predictable and the traditional, many still reflect and honor tradition, reinforcing and heightening the audience's awareness of dearly held values.

CONCLUSION: TRADITIONAL ARTS IN A RAPIDLY CHANGING WORLD

In this chapter you learned about the classical model for large-scale form and surveyed some musical changes that came about since the inception of *gong kebyar*, considering ways that tradition is maintained while allowing for innovation. Earlier in the book you saw that the patronage of the arts has undergone change since the final days of the royal Balinese courts when it was passed along to the Dutch colonial government, and then to the local *banjars* (community organizations playing for temple and other functions) and Indonesian national government institutions. While *banjar* music and dance participation remain vibrant, as does musical life in the national academies and tourist performances, other private and collective institutions also contribute to artistic life. I will end here with one such organization.

Arts Workshop/Studio Collectives (Sanggar). Many artists have recently formed home studio organizations (*sanggar*), motivated by the urge to preserve, maintain, and revive the traditional arts as well as the desire to create groups of excellence that are not limited to a local *banjar* for its membership. Often artists from various parts of Bali combine forces, or individual artists or families of artists form their own *sanggar*. They invariably encourage and teach children and youth to play *gamelan* and dance, in addition to their professional performance activities. Most Balinese children have some experience with music and dance in school, where they learn standard introductory-level repertoire. But the *sanggar* are quite different. They elevate the level of skill and creativity tremendously, with a goal to give something highly valued back to the community. Musicians tell me that contributing to the greater good of a community (*ngayah*, chapter 1), in this case by performing music and dance, is the most fulfilling sort of performance.

The family compound of Sanggar Çudamani *(pronounced* "Sudamani"*) in the summer of 2000 is a flurry of activity, with people of all ages rehearsing intently in several pavilions of the home. The organization, founded by a family of musicians, consists of a children's group (ranging in age from six to fifteen years old) and a youth group (ranging from around age sixteen to early twenties). You hear this latter group in most of the examples on this book's CD. The family is particularly well situated in the tradition, with many performance links and family ties to notable musicians and dancers of the region. Highly competent and enthusiastic, the family members have been instrumental in forming and participating in several of the best ensembles in the area.*

The leader of Sanggar Çudamani *(Dewa Putu Berata, figure 2.10) sees his role as revitalizing a community that was extremely active in the arts in former times. Dewa's generation forms a crucial link between the generation of his grandparents and future generations.*

Most musicians in Bali attribute what we might call "talent" to family heritage. In Bali, when a baby is born, some parents go to the local religious practitioner/healer to ask from which ancestor their child has been reincarnated. In this family, one of the boys was found to be a reincarnation of his grandmother, a well-known dancer. For this reason, the family says, the child is blessed with an extraordinary gift as a musician and dancer. Now an adult, he and his brothers (and a sister who is an accomplished dancer) perform together, continuing the tradition of their father, still a highly regarded musician in the community. All are phenomenal musicians as well (you heard one of Dewa Ketut Alit's compositions

here on CD track 40, and all of them play on this CD), yet they claim that it takes them much longer to learn music, and that they must work much harder at things that seem to come automatically to their brother.

This idea of some specially charged energy force that does not die but is simply transferred into another person's body reflects other aspects of the Balinese worldview and is also embodied in music: like the reincarnation cycle, old musical materials are constantly being recycled into new ones. Thus innovations are encouraged while traditions are maintained. The new has something old in it, and the past lives on in the present, just as this musician's grandmother lives on in him. The fact that she was a dancer and he is a musician further strengthens the concept of music and dance as being intrinsically linked. Musicians dance and dancers play music, even though they usually specialize in one or the other.

I went to watch the children prepare for their big performance at the Bali Arts Festival (the PKB). The gamelan *performers played like adults, with sophisticated nuances, gaya, and focused concentration. The dancers worked at their parts, closely following their coaches, who danced with them, periodically manipulating their arms, feet, or head into the desired position. I forgot I was watching children until after the rehearsal, when they immediately transformed back into playful eight- and nine-year olds.*

When you see an eight-year-old legong dancer preparing for performance it is easy to see the link she is making with generations of dancers who have undergone the same process. Likewise, the present is linked with the past in every gamelan *rehearsal. Playing at the* PKB *was to be a great honor, and the children understood this. I went to the performance, and it was outstanding. So was the group on the opposite side of the stage. Its members are sons and daughters of many of the most esteemed musicians in Denpasar, including the two sons of Nyoman Windha, the composer of* "Jagra Parwata." *The future of Balinese* gamelan *and dance performance is in the hands of the finest stewards of the arts.*

A new kind of self-awareness of the preciousness of Balinese culture has emerged for numerous reasons. Balinese culture has been the focus of anthropological writing since the Dutch period, when it was first romanticized. With tourism reaching astronomical proportions and Bali's role of cultural ambassador in an increasingly globalized Indonesia, the arts have become an enticing, sometimes compromised commodity. Beyond changes resulting from tourism are those that come with the passage of time, yielding both positive and negative results.

Time, embodied in the demon Batara Kala, who has an insatiable appetite for humans, is also honored in the performance of stories. Storytelling is central and intertwined with the embodiment of the "five powerful elements" (*panca, maha, bhuta*: earth, water, fire, air, and space), and the act of learning and preserving knowledge. There is a central belief that humans temporarily borrow these elements for life in the human realm: earth is our flesh and bones, water our bodily fluids, fire our body heat, air our breath, and space our spirit. When a person dies, these are returned to nature in the cremation and postcremation ceremonies, while the soul becomes purified and eventually a deified ancestor to be reincarnated. As my teacher, the *dalang* Pak I Nyoman Rajeg, used to say, "When a man dies, everything he has goes with him, except what he taught to someone else, little by little, over the years. When there is learning, then life goes on. When the learning stops, death wins" (Reed 1979). To return to the themes of this book, with those last comments in mind, I close in the next chapter with a visit to a cremation ceremony.

CHAPTER 7

Conclusion: Three Themes Revisited at a Cremation Ceremony

It is evident that even when musicians depart from standard models, much of the tradition is retained in Bali. The three themes central to this book support this phenomenon. Restated once more, they are: (1) the communal nature of Balinese social organization is reflected in its ensemble traditions; (2) music itself is inherently theatrical, with the ability to move a community and shape a ritual event; and (3) present-day performances link people with the past. A visit to a cremation ceremony offers one final illustration of these themes. Now you have the tools to understand what you are experiencing in this ceremony.

As an auspicious date for cremations approaches, people prepare for months ahead of time. Many village sekahas *gather together and work toward a common goal. Some build huge, ornately decorated towers, others make offerings and ceremonial food. Often a community will pool its resources and share a cremation among many families who could not afford a cremation on their own. Sometimes the dead are buried until the time that the family can afford to do the ceremony properly.*

My friends and teachers say that a cremation should be a happy occasion, and that people do not express grief, that the soul of the deceased may have a good send-off to the other world. But actually there are mixed emotions underneath the ramé *atmosphere. Grief is masked in celebration; it is a time for saying good-bye.*

This cremation was in Sukawati, a village famous for its wayang *troupes. There were at least twenty-five towers, many carrying a corpse enshrouded in white cloth. Sitting,*

FIGURE 7.1 Gender wayang *players sitting on a cremation tower in Mas, Gianyar.* (*Photo by Lisa Gold.*)

sometimes standing precariously, on some of the towers was a pair of gender wayang *players with their* genders *(figure 7.1). At the core of any ritual is the story, and the playing of* gender *on the tower links the ceremony to the* wayang *world and to the world of the ancestors. In cremations wayang plays both active and oblique parts before, during, and after the ritual. The* gender wayang *played on the towers is a reference to a familiar* Mahabharata *story that is the subtext of the ritual (see Gold 1992, 1998); as the story goes, Bima, a main character, goes to redeem his parents' souls from Batari Durga, goddess of death, thereby allowing them to enter heaven. The procession to the death temple would follow a similar path, as the family of the deceased must also honor Durga to ensure the soul's safe passage.*

Standing ready at this cremation were numerous balaganjur *groups, one to be played in the procession with each tower. Spatial orientation is clearly observed: the* gender wayang *are elevated, communicating with the spirit world as it guides the soul, while the* balaganjur *are firmly on the ground with the people in the procession and warding off evil spirits.*

There was an uncanny silence, rare in Bali, as people gathered at high noon, after which all cremations must begin. This is the time when the demon Batara Kala (fittingly, symbolic of time) lurks at village intersections, ready to devour his prey. The balaganjur *music is thought to entertain him, though some say it wards away evil. Others say its main purpose is to incite the crowd and enable the bearers of the towers to carry their heavy load all the way to the cremation grounds.*

At a signal the first balaganjur *group begins playing, and suddenly an atmosphere of wild chaos seems to come over the crowd. The loud gongs, cymbals, drums, and gong-chimes instantly transform the mood from quiet expectation to wild celebration, from underlying tension to cathartic release. As the procession winds its way to the death temple there is a jumble of sounds: the* balaganjur *processional piece is a* gilak *gong pattern with a syncopated* kempur *pattern (CD track 9, activity 5.6); the* gender *musicians play other pieces that are inaudible to the crowd, underscoring the conceptual importance of guiding the soul; the crowd cheers and yells as many people carry each tower, swaying and moving through the narrow hilly road. At each intersection they stop and twirl the tower to confuse the evil spirits that lurk at intersections. They cross a precarious bamboo bridge over a deep ravine. A* dalang *standing on the tower throws ancient Chinese coins while reciting* mantras *at certain points along the way. In a way this ritual is being accompanied and narrated as a dramatic performance would be, as it follows the path of the story of Bima's journey.*

Upon reaching the graveyard the towers seem to float above the crowd as I get pushed into an irrigation ditch among hundreds of people. By the side of the road one balaganjur *group*

stops and takes advantage of a lull in the procession before the next tower arrives. They have been practicing a new kind of balaganjur *known as* kreasi balaganjur *("new creations for* balaganjur*"). They squat by the road and play a new arrangement that is much more complex than the* gilak *they had been playing earlier. It is multisectional, with a long, slow* pangawak *(CD track 10). These musicians had clearly been practicing and were excited to show off. In the midst of this ancient ritual there is room for the contemporary. A small crowd gathers to listen and admire.*

The towers are lowered to the ground near the death temple, and the enshrouded corpses are placed inside wooden sarcophagi carved in the form of bulls and other animals and decorated with velvet and gold. Then they and the towers are lit on fire. As smoke fills the air, gamelan angklung *plays in the cremation grounds. It is said to have melancholy associations (CD track 41 is an* angklung *excerpt taken from another kind of ceremony). People are tired, and the mood has shifted drastically from earlier that day. My teachers say that the* slendro *tuning of the* gender *and* angklung, *now permeating the air and mingling with smoke, is fitting to escort the soul to the spirit world, while the* pelog *tuning of the* balaganjur *heard earlier is better for communicating with demons and humans. Sound has specific meaning and power.*

As we get in the car to drive home, I look at the offering on the dashboard with its freshly lit incense and I remember the TV placed with all the other offerings at a ceremony I attended (figure 7.2). I think of a time when I asked someone why she was giving offerings to certain electrical appliances in the kitchen but not to others, and her reply: "Because it has always been that way."

This is the idea of tradition's encompassing and adapting to modern life. The past is treasured and honored, but not at the expense of the present needs in a changing world. Change is readily accepted, while past traditions are valued and retained at the core of the innovative.

FIGURE 7.2 *TV with offerings at a ceremony.* (Photo by Lisa Gold.)

Glossary

adat tradition, encompassing religion (for which there is now a distinct Indonesian term, *agama*), divine cosmic and social order, and all community activities.

aerophone instrument in which sound is produced by a vibrating column of air.

angsel cue, sign, or articulation of a dance movement and music marked by a sudden rhythmic break or accent.

babad historical chronicles enacted in *topeng* plays.

balé banjar community center structure and meeting center where gamelan is often rehearsed.

Bali Aga pre-Hindu Balinese communities.

bonang pitched, horizontally played bossed gongs (term from Java), also called *gong-chimes.*

boss raised portion of the gong that is struck.

chordophone instrument in which the sound is produced by a vibrating string.

colotomic (from the Greek term for "divide") punctuating framework and metric emphasis provided by the gongs.

condong female attendant to the princess in *legong* and *gambuh;* she is both character and stock character *type.*

dalang shadow puppet master.

Denpasar the capital city of Bali.

desa, kala, patra place, time, circumstance.

empat "four"; describes the interval spanning four keys/pitches.

gambangan a section of a piece using the 5 + 3 stress pattern of *gamelan gambang*, now come to mean the final section in a *kebyar* piece.

gambelan (from *magambel*, "to strike") Balinese term for *gamelan.*

gamelan Balinese or Javanese musical ensembles, mainly idiophones, sometimes flutes and membranophones (see text for details).

gamelan angklung a small ensemble tuned to a four-tone *slendro*-derived tuning, often used to accompany death rites and other ceremonies; it is one of the most commonly found ensembles in Bali and is used for all occasions.

gamelan balaganjur processional (marching) *gamelan* of gongs, cymbals, and drums.

gamelan bebonangan a form of *gamelan balaganjur.*

gamelan gambang a seven-tone, sacred, pre-Hindu Balinese ensemble of 4 xylophones and 2 sarons.

gamelan gambuh dance drama and *gamelan* from which many genres are derived; melody is played on large vertical bamboo flutes

gamelan gender wayang a quartet of ten-keyed metallophones that accompanies the shadow play and some rituals.

gamelan gong gedé ("*gamelan* of the large gong") ceremonial large, bronze ensemble from the Middle Period courts and temple.

gamelan gong kebyar *gamelan* developed in the early twentieth century with the "explosive" sound.

gamelan palegongan bronze ensemble that accompanies legong, metallphones, drums, flutes and rebab, led by 2 *gender rambat.*

gamelan semar pagulingan a court *gamelan*, originally in a seven-tone tuning and played in the king's bedchamber.

gangsa jongkok metallophone with ("squatting") removable keys slid onto nails that sit on trough resonator, used in gong gedé.

gaya charisma, flashy demeanor.

gedé large, great.

gender rambat a pelog-tuned metallophone with fifteen keys suspended over bamboo resonators played with a pair of hard mallets in palegongan.

gender wayang see *gamelan gender wayang*.

genderan section of a piece emulating *gender* music.

gentorak bell-tree, used in *legong* and other delicate courtly ensembles.

gineman a metrically free prelude.

grantangan Balinese notation system based on vowel sounds: *nding, ndong, ndeng, ndung, ndang* (abbr. *i o e u a*).

halus refined character type.

heterophony "different voices"; musical texture of one melody performed almost simultaneously and somewhat differently by multiple musicians; usually there is a nuclear melody (either played on some instrument or as a conceptual framework in the minds of the musicians) on which other parts play an abstraction or elaboration; there may be several equally important melodies at once.

idiophone an instrument in which the primary sound-producing body is the material of the instrument itself.

juru tandak a trained *dalang* acting as a master narrator in dance dramas.

kaja and kelod, kangin and kauh the cardinal directions on Bali: toward the (sacred) mountain and toward the sea, east and west respectively; because the mountains are toward the center of the island, *kaja* and *kelod* vary according to where in Bali the speaker is; *kangin* and *kelod* are always east and west.

kajar a timekeeping, horizontal gong with a sunken boss, played with a wooden beater, with three musical functions: plays beat, divides a phrase, or plays a composite of the two drum patterns.

kasar coarse character type.

Kawi Old Javanese language.

kawitan an introductory section of a piece (the "head").

kayon tree-of-life puppet in shadow play

kebyar onomatopoetic term for the explosive sound of a twentieth-century musical style.

kecak vocalized form of *gamelan* consisting of men chanting the syllable *cak* (pronounced "chak") in interlocking parts while others sing melody, beat, and gong parts; Now a form of dance drama enacting the *Ramayana*, it is known as the "Monkey Chant" because the people chanting *cak* take on the role of the monkey armies.

kekawin sung poetry in the Old Javanese (Kawi) language.

keras strong character type.

kidung ceremonial chant in Javanese meter.

kompak describes a "tight" ensemble.

kotekan interlocking parts (also called *candatan* and *ubitan*).

kreasi baru ("new creations") pieces composed in the twentieth century and today for *gong kebyar.*

lalambatan ("slow music") long compositions played in temple ceremonies, traditionally on *gamelan gong gede.*

legong a "classical" Balinese dance form with three prepubescent girls, often involving trance.

Mahabharata Indian-derived Hindu epic told in Balinese and Javanese performing arts.

mantra sacred, magical syllables and invocations, often silent, in the Sanskrit language, originating from India.

membranophone instrument in which the primary sound-producing body is a membrane stretched over a resonator or frame.

metallophone instrument in which the primary sound-producing body is metal keys.

mudra Indian symbolic hand gestures used in dance and by Brahmana priests.

ngayah selfless contribution to a ceremony (includes dance and musical performance), similar to offering.

norot neighbor-tone *kotekan.*

notasi KOKAR notational system developed and used at the KOKAR music conservatory (now called SMKI).

nyog-cag ("leaping") type of *kotekan.*

ocak-ocakan *reyong* technique of playing percussively on the rim of the kettle with the wooden part of the mallet, alternately with striking a chord on the boss.

odalan temple ceremony commemorating the anniversary of a temple.

ombak waves, as in the sea and the undulations of paired tuning and of the acoustic beating of the gong.

oral formulaity spontaneous compositional process in which memorized formulas and parts are put together on the spot by a performer, used in storytelling and other orally transmitted art forms.

ostinato a short, repeating melodic or rhythmic pattern.

paired tuning instruments tuned in pairs with one slightly higher than the other so that when struck together the sound produced pulsates.

pancayadnya five ceremonial categories.

panggul mallet.

panyacah mid-sized metallophone.

pamero two "extra" tones, outside of the pentatonic modes.

pangawak ("main body") of a piece: the longest section.

pangecet ("feet") short, compressed, final section of a piece; *kebyar* pieces may have more than one *pangecet*.

Pesta Kesenian Bali (PKB) annual Bali Arts Festival.

pengumbang the "exhaler" or "hummer" instrument in paired tuning.

pengisep the "inhaler" or "sucker" instrument in paired tuning.

pentatonic five-tone scale.

pokok the basic melodic part, skeleletal melody.

polos ("basic, simple") the half of *kotekan* usually on the beat, closest to the *pokok;* cf. *sangsih.*

polyphony musical texture in which two or more independent melodic lines are played or sung simultaneously and contrapuntally; *stratified polyphony* occurs in *gamelan*: the musical layers are hierarchical in register and rhythmic density.

Ramayana Indian-derived Hindu epic told in Balinese and Javanese performing arts.

ramé boisterous, full atmosphere, an essential requirement in ceremonies.

repertoires groups of pieces that are linked in some way.

sanggar arts collectives.

sangsih ("differing") the half of *kotekan* usually off the beat; cf. *polos.*

Sanskrit ancient Indian language used by Balinese Brahmana priests.

saron metallophone with keys that sit on a trough resonator played with a hard mallet.

sarong cloth wrapped around lower body in traditional dress.

sekaha community organization, as in a *gamelan sekaha.*

sekala* and *niskala the seen (visible) and the unseen (invisible) realms, respectively.

seledet eye movement.

selisir the most prevalent pentatonic tuning system or mode, using pitches 1 2 3 5 6 of the *pelog* scale.

semar pagulingan see *gamelan semar pagulingan.*

Semara love deity.

sendratari dance drama, an acronym of *seni* = art, drama, and *tari* = dance.

sip describes a tight musical group.

slit-drum hollowed out wooden log that is struck with a stick.

sloka ancient Sanskrit poetry.

soundscape all sounds heard as they mingle together.

stratified polyphony see *polyphony.*

suka duka happy together, sad together.

syncopated stress in the rhythm that counters the regularly stressed beats implied by the meter or pulse.

tabuh lepas "free composition" with no dramatic or programmatic association.

taksu divine inspiration that overcomes a dancer or *dalang* during performance.

tari lepas "free dance" with no dramatic or programmatic association.

tekep, patut,* or *patet mode (tekep = lit., the covering of holes on the *gambuh* flute).

wayang kulit shadow puppet theater or puppets made of rawhide.

worldview all aspects of physical, psychological, cosmological, and philosophical views that contribute to the way a society understands the world.

References

Anonymous. n.d. *Aji gurnita*. Unpublished manuscript (approx. 19th century).

Bandem, I Made. 1983. "The Evolution of Legong from Sacred to Secular Dance of Bali." In Betty True Jones, ed., *Dance as a Cultural Heritage*; 113–19. New York: Congress on Research in Dance, Inc.

Bandem, I Made, ed. 1988. *Prakempa: Sebuah lontar gambelan Bali*. Denpasar: STSI.

Becker, Judith. 1979. "Time and Tune in Java." In Aram A. Yengoyan and A.L. Becker, eds., *The Imagination of Reality: Essays in Southeast Asian Coherence Systems*, 197–210. Norwood, New Jersey: Albex Publishing Company.

———. 1981. "A Musical Icon: Power and Meaning in Javanese Gamelan Music." In Wendy Steiner, ed., *The Sign in Music and Literature*, 203–15. Austin: University of Texas Press.

———. 1993. *Gamelan Stories: Tantrism, Islam, and Aesthetics in Central Java*. Monographs in Southeast Asian Studies. Phoenix: Program for Southeast Asian Studies, Arizona State University.

Boon, James. 1974. "The Progress of the Ancestors in a Balinese Temple Group (Pre-1906–1972)." *Journal of Asian Studies* 34:7–25.

———. 1977. *The Anthropological Romance of Bali, 1597–1972: Dynamic Perspectives in Marriage and Caste, Politics and Religion*. Cambridge Studies in Cultural Systems. Cambridge: Cambridge University Press.

———. 1986. "Symbols, Sylphs, and Siwa; Allegorical Machineries in the Text of Balinese Culture." In Victor W. Turner and Edward M. Bruner, eds.; *The Anthropology of Experience*, 239–60. Urbana: University of Illinois Press.

Brinner, Benjamin. 1995. *Knowing Music, Making Music: Javanese Gamelan and the Theory of Musical Competence and Interaction*. Chicago: University of Chicago Press.

Crapanzano, Vincent. 1986. "Hermes' Dilema: The Masking of Subversion in Ethnographic Description." In James Clifford and George E. Marcus, eds., *Writing Culture: The Poetics and Politics of Ethnography*, 51–76. Berkeley and Los Angeles: University of California Press.

Daniel, Ana. Bali Behind the Mask. 1981. New York: Alfred A. Knopf, Inc.

Dibia, I Wayan, and Sue DeVale. 1991. "Sekar Anyar: An Exploration of Meaning in Balinese Gamelan." *World of Music* 33/1:5–52.

Emigh, John. 1979. "Playing with the Past: Visitation and Illusion in the Mask Theatre of Bali." *Drama Review* 23/2:1–36.

Geertz, Clifford. 1980. *Negara: The Theatre State in Nineteenth-Century Bali*. Princeton, N.J.: Princeton University Press.

Geertz, Clifford, and Hildred Geertz. 1975. *Kinship in Bali*. Chicago: University of Chicago Press.

Harnish, David. 1991. "Music at the Lingsar Temple Festival: The Encapsulation of Meaning in the Balinese/Sasak Interface in Lombok, Indonesia." Ph.D. diss. University of California at Los Angeles.

Hobart, Mark. 1978. "The Path of the Soul: The Legitimacy of Nature in Balinese Conceptions of Space." in G. B. Milner, ed., *Natural Symbols in Southeast Asia*, 5–28. London: School of Oriental and African Studies, University of London.

Lansing, Stephen J. 1979. "The Formation of the Court-Village Axis in the Balinese Arts." In Edward Bruner and Judith Becker, eds., *Art, Ritual, and Society in Indonesia*, Ohio University. Center for International Studies Southeast Asia Series 53:10–30.

McPhee, Colin. 1936. "The Balinese Wajang Koelit and its Music." *Djawa* 16:1–50. Reprint in Belo 1981 (see "Resources").

Picard, Michel. 1996 *Bali: Cultural Tourism and Touristic Culture*. Singapore: Archipelago Press.

Schaareman, Danker. 1980. "The Gamelan Gambang of Tatulingga, Bali." *Ethnomusicology* 26/3:465–82.

———. 1986. *Tatulingga: Tradition and Continuity: An Investigation in Ritual and Social Organization in Bali*. Basler Beitrage zur ethnologie 24. Base; Ethnologisches Seminar der Universität und Museum fur Volkerkunde.

———. 1992. "The Shining of the Deity: Selunding Music of Tatulingga (Karangasem) and its Ritual Use." *In* Dankar Schaareman, ed., *Balinese Music in Context: A Sixty-Fifth Birthday Tribute to Hans Oesch*. Forum Ethnomusicologicum 4: 173–94. Basel Studien Zur Ethnomusicologie. Basel: Amadeus.

Spies, Walter, and Beryl de Zoete. 2002. *Dance and Drama in Bali*. London: Faber & Faber, 1938. Reprint. Hong Kong: Periplus.

Sweeney, Amin. 1972. *The Ramayana and the Malay Shadow-Play*. Kuala Lumpur: National University of Malaysia Press.

———. 1980. *Authors and Audiences in Traditional Malay Literature*. Berkeley: Center for South and Southeast Asia Studies, University of California.

———. 1987. *A Full Hearing: Orality and Literacy in the Malay World*. Berkeley and Los Angeles: University of California Press.

———. 1991. "Literacy and Epic in the Malay World." In Joyce Flueckiger Burkhalter and Laurie J. Sears, eds., *Boundaries of the Text: Epic Performances in South and Southeast Asia*. Michigan Papers on South and Southeast Asia. Ann Arbor: University of Michigan Center for South and Southeast Asian Studies.

Vickers, Adrian H. 1985. "The Realm of the Senses: Images of the Court Music of Pre-Colonial Bali." *Imago Musicae* 2:143–77.

———. 1986. "The Desiring Prince: A Study of the Kidung Malat as Text." Ph.D. thesis. University of Sydney.

———. 1992. "Kidung Meters and the Interpretation of the Malat." In Dankar Schaareman, ed., *Balinese Music in Context: A Sixty-Fifth Birthday Tribute to Hans Oesch.* Forum Ethnomusicologicum 4:221–43. Basel Studien zur Ethnomusicologie. Basel: Amadeus.

Vonck, Henrice M. 1995. "The Music of the North Balinese Shadow Play: The Dramatic Function of Gender Wayang in Tejakula." In W. Van Zanten and M Van Roon, eds., *The Performing Arts World-wide: Ethnomusicology in the Netherlands: Present Situation and Traces of the Past,* special issue, *Oideion* 2:145–171.

———. 1997. "Manis and Keras in Image, Word, and Music of Wayang Kulit in Tejakula, North-Bali." Ph.D. diss. University of Amsterdam.

Wikan, Unni. 1990. *Managing Turbulent Hearts: A Balinese Formula for Living.* Chicago: University of Chicago Press.

Wiratini, Ni Made. 1991. "Condong and Its Roles in Balinese Dance-Drama." M.A. thesis. University of California at Los Angeles.

Zurbuchen, Mary Sabina. 1987. *The Language of Balinese Shadow Theater.* Princeton, N.J.: Princeton University Press.

———. 1991. "Palm Leaf and Performance: The Epics in Balinese Theater." In Joyce Fluckiger Burkhalter and Laurie J. Sears, eds., *Boundaries of the Text: Epic Performances in South and Southeast Asia.* Michigan Papers on South and Southeast Asia 35. Ann Arbor: University of Michigan Center for South and Southeast Asia Studies.

Resources

Reading

Bakan, Michael. 1999. *Music of Death and New Creation: Experiences in the World of Balinese Gamelan Beleganjur*. Chicago: University of Chicago Press.

Bandem, I Made, and Frederik E. deBoer. 1995. *Balinese Dance in Transition: Kaja and Kelod*. 2d ed. Kuala Lumpur: Oxford University Press.

Belo, Jane. 1949. *Rangda and Barong*. Monographs of the American Ethnological Society 16 Seattle: University of Washington Press.

———. 1960. *Trance in Bali*. New York: Columbia University Press.

———, ed. 1981. *Traditional Balinese Culture*. New York: Columbia University Press, 1970. Reprint.

Dibia, I Wayan, Rucina Ballinger, and Barbara Anello. 2004. *Balinese Dance, Drama and Music*. Singapore: Periplus Editors.

Covarrubias, Miguel. 1953. *Island of Bali*. New York: Putnam.

Dibia, I Wayan. 1985. "Odalan of Hindu-Bali: A Religious Festival, a Social Occasion, and a Theatrical Event." *Asian Theatre Journal* 2/1:61–65.

———. 1992. "Arja: A Sung Dance-Drama of Bali: A Study of Change and Transformation." Ph.D. diss. University of California at Los Angeles.

———. 1996. *Kecak. The Vocal Chant of Bali*. Bali: Hartanto Art Books.

Eiseman, Fred, Jr. 1989. *Sekala and Niskala*. 3 vols. Berkeley, Calif.: Periplus.

Gold, Lisa. 1992. "Musical Expression in the Wayang Repertoire: A Bridge between Narrative and Ritual." In Dankar Schaareman, ed., *Balinese Music in Context: A Sixty-Fifth Birthday Tribute to Hans Oesch*. Forum Ethnomusicologicum 4:245–75. Basel Studien zur Ethnomusicologie. Basel: Amadeus.

———. 1998. "The Gender Wayang Repertoire in Theater and Ritual." Ph.D. diss. University of California at Berkeley.

———. 2001. "Indonesia: Bali." *New Grove Dictionary of Music and Musicians*. 2d ed. London: Macmillan.

Harnish, David. 1998. "Bali." In Sean Williams and Terry Miller, eds., *The Garland Encyclopedia of World Music.* Vol. 4. *Southeast Asia*, 729–962.

Herbst, Edward. 1997. *Voices in Bali: Energies and Perceptions in Vocal Music and Dance Theater.* Hanover, N.H.: Wesleyan University Press.

Hobart, Angela. 1987. *Dancing Shadows of Bali: Theatre and Myth.* London: KPI.

Holt, Claire. 1967. *Art in Indonesia: Continuities and Change.* Ithaca, N.Y.: Cornell University Press.

Lansing, Stephen J. 1983. *The Three Worlds of Bali.* Westport, Conn.: Praeger.

McPhee, Colin. 1966. *Music in Bali.* New Haven, Conn.: Yale University Press.

Picard, Michel. 1990. " 'Cultural Tourism' in Bali: Cultural Performances as Tourist Attraction." *Indonesia* 49/April: 37–74.

Rai, I Wayan. 1996. "Balinese *Gambelan Semar Pegulingan Saih Pitu:* The Modal System." Ph.D. diss., University of Maryland, Baltimore County.

Tenzer, Michael. 1991. *Balinese Music.* Singapore: Periplus.

———. 2000. *Gamelan Gong Kebyar: The Art of Twentieth-Century Balinese Music.* Chicago: University of Chicago Press.

Toth, Andrew. 1980. *Recordings of the Traditional Music of Bali and Lombok.* Society for Ethnomusicology Special Series 4. N.p.: Society for Ethnomusicology.

Vickers, Adrian H. 1989. *Bali: A Paradise Created.* Berkeley, Calif.: Periplus.

Vitale, Wayne. 1990. "Kotekan: The Technique of Interlocking Parts in Balinese Music." *Balungan* 4/2:2–15.

———. 1996. Liner notes. *Music of the Gamelan Gong Kebyar: Works by I Nyoman Windha.* Vital Records CD 402.

———. 2002. "Balinese *Kebyar* Music Breaks the Five-Tone Barrier: New Compositions for Seven-Tone *Gamelan.*" *Perspectives of New Music* 40/1:5–69.

Wallis, Richard. 1980. "The Voice as a Mode of Cultural Expression in Bali." Ph.D. diss. University of Michigan.

Listening

Bakan, Michael. 1999. 2 CDs enclosed in book (above reference).

Bali: Balinese Music of Lombok. 1997. Recorded by David Harnish. Anthology of Traditional Music AUVIDIS D 8272.

Bali: Gamelan and Kecak. 1989. Recorded in Bali by David Lewiston. 1989. Elektra/Nonesuch Explorer Series 9 79204-2.

Bali: Music of the Wayang Kulit I and II. 1983. Tokyo: JVC VICG-5266-2.

Bali: Musique pour le Gong Gede de Batur. 1972. Ocora C559002.

Çudamani: The Seven-Tone Gamelan Orchestra from the Village of Pengosekan, Bali. 2002. Vital Records 440.

Gamelan Batel Wayang Ramayana. Recorded in Sading, Bali, 1989. Liner notes by I Nyoman Wenten. CMP Records CD3003.

Gamelan Gong Gede of Batur Temple. 1990. King Records, KICC 5153.

Gamelan Music from Sebatu: Sacred music from Sebatu. 1972. Archiv Produktion 2533 130.

Gamelan Sekar Jaya: Balinese Music in America. 1995. El Cerrito, Calif. 6485 Conlon Avenue, El Cerrito, CA 94530.

Gamelan Sekar Jaya: Fajar: Balinese Performing Arts in America. 1999. El Cerrito, Calif.

Gamelan Semar Pegulingan: Gamelan of the Love God. 1972. Notes by Robert E. Brown and Philip B. Yampolsky. Nonesuch Explorer Series H 72046.

Gamelan Semar Pegulingan of Binoh Village. 1992. World music library 55. Tokyo: King Records, Seven Seas, King KICC 5155

Gamelan Semar Pegulingan Saih Pitu: The Heavenly Orchestra of Bali. 1991. CMP Records 3008.

Jegog: The Bamboo Gamelan of Bali, Performed by Werdi Sentana. 1991. CMP Records 3011.

Gender Wayang of Sukawati Village. 1990.World Music Library. King Records KICC 5156.

Living Art, Sounding Spirit: The Bali Sessions. 1999. Produced by Micky Hart. RCD 10449.

Music for the Gods. 1994. Fahnestock South Sea expedition, Indonesia endangered music project. Salem, Mass.: Rykodisc RCD 10315.

Music from the Morning of the World. 2003. New York: Nonesuch Explorer Series H 72015. (1967 1st release)

Music for the Balinese Shadow Play: Gender Wayang from Teges Kanginan, Pliatan, Bali. 1967. Notes by Robert E. Brown Nonesuch Explorer Series H 72037.

Music of Bali: Gamelan, Gender Wayang. 1982. Performed by Wayan Loceng and Ketut Balik. Recorded in the village of Sukawati. New York: Lyrichord LLST 7360.

Music of Bali: Gamelan Semar Pegulingan from the Village of Ketewel. Recorded in Bali by Wayne Vitale. New York: Lyrichord. LYRCD 7408.

Music of the Gambuh Theater. 1999. Vital Records 501.

Music of the Gamelan Gong Kebyar, Vol 1. Performed by musicians from STSI Denpasar. Vital Records 401.

Music of the Gamelan Gong Kebyar. Vol. 2. *Works of I Nyoman Windha, Performed by Three Award-Winning Gamelan Orchestras from Villages in Bali.* 1996. Vital Records 402.

Tenzer, Michael. 2000. 2 CDs enclosed in book (above reference).

The Roots of Gamelan: The First Recordings: Bali, 1928, New York, 1941. 1999. World Arbiter 2001.

Viewing

Shadow Puppetry and Culture Video Recordings

Reed, C. L. *Shadowmaster*. 1981. San Francisco: Shadowlight Productions.

The Three Worlds of Bali. 1981. Produced and directed by Ira R. Abrams, written by Ira R. Abrams and J. Stephen Lansing. Odyssey no. 208.

Legong, Baris, Calonrang, Kecak

Bali beyond the Postcard. 1991. Nancy Dine, executive producer, Peggy Stern, director. New York: Filmakers Library.

Bali: Mask of Rangda. 198?. Cos Cob, Conn.: Hartley Film Foundation.

Dance and Trance of Balinese Children. 1995. Produced and directed by Madeleine Richeport-Haley and Jay Haley. Additional footage from films made by Gregory Bateson and Margaret Mead in 1936–39. New York: Triangle Productions/Filmakers Library.

Island of Temples. 1990. Directed by Deben Bhattacharya, produced by Seabourne Enterprises (Film Productions). London: Sussex Tapes; Guilford, Conn.: distributed in the U.S. and Canada by Video-Forum, a division of Jeffrey Norton Publishers.

JVC Video Anthology of World Music and Dance. Vol. 9 and 10. *Bali*.

Trance and Dance in Bali. [1952] 1991. Photography by Gregory Bateson and Jane Belo, written and narrated by Margaret Mead. University Park, Pa.: Distributed by Audio-Visual Services, Pennsylvania State University.

Index

The letter *a* following a page number denotes an activity. The letter *f* denotes a figure.